D0953385

HILLSBORO PUBLIC LIBRARIES
Hillsboro, OR
Member of Washington County
COOPERATIVE LIBRARY SERVICES

A Recipe 4 Robbery

by Marybeth Kelsey

Greenwillow Books
An Imprint of HarperCollinsPublishers

HILLSBORO PUBLIC LIBRARIES
Hillsboro, OR
Member of Washington County
COOPERATIVE LIBRARY SERVICES

This book is a work of fiction. References to real people, events, establishments, organizations, or locales are intended only to provide a sense of authenticity, and are used to advance the fictional narrative. All other characters, and all incidents and dialogue, are drawn from the author's imagination and are not to be construed as real.

A Recipe for Robbery
Copyright © 2009 by Marybeth Kelsey
All rights reserved. No part of this book may be used or reproduced in any manner whatsoever without written permission except in the case of brief quotations embodied in critical articles and reviews. Printed in the United States of America. For information address HarperCollins Children's Books, a division of HarperCollins Publishers, 10 East 53rd Street, New York 10022.
www.harpercollinschildrens.com

The text of this book is set in Berkeley Medium.
Book design by Sylvie Le Floc'h

Library of Congress Cataloging-in-Publication Data

Kelsey, Marybeth.
A recipe for robbery / by Marybeth Kelsey.
p. cm.
"Greenwillow Books."
Summary: An unsupervised goose, missing family heirlooms, and some suspicious characters turn the annual cucumber festival into a robbery investigation for three sixth-grade friends.
ISBN 978-0-06-128843-2 (trade bdg.) — ISBN 978-0-06-128845-6 (lib. bdg.)
[1. Mystery and detective stories. 2. Festivals—Fiction. 3. Community life—Fiction.] I. Title.
PZ7.K302Re 2009   [Fic]—dc22   2008029145

09 10 11 12 13 LP/RRDB First Edition 10 9 8 7 6 5 4 3 2 1

 Greenwillow Books

41255406   10/09

To my guys:
Terry, Max, Eric, and Christopher

With thanks to Bloomington,
Indiana, musician Tom Roznowski,
whose song "Stewed Cucumbers"
inspired this book.

Contents

cu*cum*ber (kyoo kum ber) *n*. 1. a creeping plant, *Cucumis sativus*, occurring in many cultivated forms. 2. the edible, fleshy, usually long, cylindrical fruit of this vine. 3. a member of the kingdom Plantae and the class Magnoliopsida, primarily devoured in the *fresh*, or *pickled* form, and recently deemed unfit for human consumption in the *cooked*, or *stewed* form by me, Lindy Lou Phillips.

Chapter 1
Veggie-licious . . . (Not)

"Yuck!" I nudged my best friend, Margaret, and pointed to a bowl on the serving table in front of us. Long, wrinkled greenish things were floating in some kind of thick sauce.

Margaret's eyes widened. "What is that stuff?"

I lifted the lid for a better look. A glob of sauce oozed down the side of the bowl and onto the tablecloth. It looked like a mixture of curdled milk and motor oil.

"It's something one of the Tarts made," I whispered. That's my mom's cooking club—the Bloomsberry Tarts, to be exact. It's named for our little town of

Bloomsberry, Florida, also known as the Cucumber Capital of the World.

Every June the Tarts help organize the Bloomsberry Cucumber Festival in honor of our local vegetable and fruit farmers. The club's members whip up gobs of veggie dishes for the big event, and some of them even dress in vegetable costumes and ride in the Main Street parade—like my mom. An hour ago, she'd been the carrot riding on my dad's fire truck. Dad and my six-year-old brother, Henry, had been on the truck with her, dressed like beets.

Up until this year I'd always played along.

"You ready to become a radish, Lindy?" my dad had asked earlier that morning. He'd just come out of the bathroom, and his hands were dark red from the gel he'd used to color his and Henry's hair. "Your mom has the costume ready."

I'd stared at him for a couple of seconds, tongue-tied. I didn't want to make my dad feel bad, but I'd been plotting for a while on how to get out of this family tradition. "Uh, well, Margaret and I were kind of planning to, um—"

"Lindy says it's dumb to dress up like vegetables," Henry called from the bathroom. "She's not gonna do it this year. She says you and Mom will have to tie her up and drag her with you before she—"

"Those were *not* my exact words," I'd said. "And how come you were eavesdropping on my private phone conversation, anyway?"

Dad just laughed. "It's okay, kiddo. Guess you've finally outgrown the costume thing, huh?" He'd been right about that. No other sixth grader in Bloomsberry (that I knew of, anyway) wanted to ride the Sizzler in a smothering hot radish costume.

After watching the parade and checking out the midway rides, all Margaret and I had in mind was finding the perfect lunch: corn dogs, french fries, and strawberry shortcake. But those lines were already a mile long, so we'd decided to cruise the main food tent to see what else looked good. That's how we'd ended up at the Tarts' serving table; it was the only one without a line. My mom had even made a giant sign that said, FREE! VEGGIE-LICIOUS TREATS FROM OUR TARTS TO YOUR HEARTS, but so far only a few people had trickled over to check it out.

Margaret leaned toward the motor oil casserole. She pinched her nose and glanced back up at me. Her eyes were crossed. "Oh, gross. It's sour cream. Quick! Put the lid back on."

I should've taken her advice. Instead, I stuck my face within an inch of the muck. So close I could count the peppercorns on top of it. *Whew.* I nearly passed out.

"Hey, I know what this is," I said. "It's cream of alien fingers, sautéed over worms and—"

"Go ahead!" boomed a woman's voice from behind us. "Try some of it, girls."

I spun around, nearly swallowing my tonsils as a two-hundred-pound cucumber shoved her way through a couple of Tarts and a farmer-looking guy and barreled toward me. A fat, long-necked goose waddled at her heels. I knew right away this particular cucumber was Mrs. Evelyn Unger, the wacky old lady who lives near our school and collects more stray animals than Barbie has bikinis. It's because of the pet goose she's always got tagging along that we kids call her Granny Goose.

Before I had a chance to get away, Granny Goose took a ladle and dumped three heaping mounds of the stuff on my plate. We're talking a Mount Everest of mushy crud.

"These are my swamp-dilly-scrumptious stewed cucumbers," she said, grinning at me. "That sauce bubbled in my Crock-Pot all night long. It's one of my best recipes. Pickles here adores it. Don't you, love?" She tugged at the leash in her hand, and her goose honked.

Then she leaned toward me, dropping her voice like we were undercover FBI agents working a top secret case. "But I want human opinions, if you know what I mean. I can't really trust a goose, for goodness' sake." She thumped me on the back and hooted with laughter before going on. "Listen up. I'm entering this recipe in the Florida Fruit and Vegetable Cook-off, and I need to know if all my ingredients complement the cucumbers. So after you eat it, give it to me straight, honey. Is it too heavy on the mushroom paste?"

Mushroom paste? Whoa. I had to swallow twice to keep my breakfast of Fruity Bears from crawling back up my throat. I turned to Margaret for help, but she wasn't standing beside me anymore. She'd already moved to the far end of the table and was helping herself to some mashed potatoes.

I squirmed under Granny Goose's smiling gaze, secretly plotting what I could do with her cucumbers. Just when I decided to accidentally trip and spill them all, I noticed my mother—otherwise known as Miss Perfect Manners—standing on the other side of the serving table with Henry. I groaned. Mom still had on her carrot costume, and the steely gleam in her eyes warned me she was totally into this vegetable thing.

I really couldn't risk making my mom mad, because I planned on begging her for something huge later that evening. So I took a deep breath and smiled at Granny Goose. "Er . . . thank you very much, Mrs. Unger. This sure does look interesting. I'll let you know about the mushroom paste."

"Yes, and it smells delightful," Mom said.

Oh, yeah? I thought. Since when does fungus smell anything but raunchy?

"I'm sure Lindy will enjoy a few of these cucumbers before her *dessert*," Mom said. "Isn't that right, dear?" She helped herself to a microscopic spoonful, then dribbled some onto Henry's plate. His eyes rounded with alarm, like he'd just been handed a hornets' nest. But when he started to whine, Mom gave him the Look.

I covered my mouth and snickered, thinking

how funny it was that Henry, who always whined his way out of eating anything but chicken nuggets or macaroni, had finally got stuck with a vegetable.

He scrunched his eyes at me, and Mom must've heard my smothered laugh, because that's when I got an even sterner version of the Look. Now, if you knew the Carrot, you'd know the Look meant this: "Do not even think of spilling those cucumbers, Lindy Lou Phillips, if you want to live to see your twelfth birthday."

If I was going to get rid of the cukes, I'd have to be tricky about it.

Chapter 2

If It Wasn't for Henry's Balloon Hat . . .

I couldn't chance getting caught throwing Granny Goose's food away. Not today, anyway. I'd been doing all kinds of things to impress my mom for the last couple of weeks—stuff like cleaning lint out of the dryer, fluffing the pillows on her bed, and taking out the trash without being asked. I'd scrubbed the gunk from under the toilet seat, too, even though it made me gag the whole time. I figured the more mature and cheerful I acted, and the more I pointed out all the helpful things I'd done, the better chance I'd have of changing her mind about my going to summer band camp with Margaret.

Granny Goose leaned down to adjust Pickles's collar. I said a quick good-bye and started backing away, but I didn't get far. Mom was right behind me. She was talking to her hairdresser, Cricket, about how a trim would "accentuate the auburn highlights" in my dark brown hair.

"See what I mean?" Mom said, brushing the bangs off my forehead.

Both Cricket and the tall blond guy with her eyed my hair as if it were a clump of seaweed. "Yeah, she could use a cut all right," Cricket said. "Send her in. We'll get those dead ends off."

"Well, it's not just the dead ends. I'd like it styled, and I want all that shaggy mess out of her eyes," Mom said. "They're Lindy's best feature. She's the only one in the family with hazel eyes, and you can't see them with that hair hanging. . . . " Blah, blah, blah.

She yammered on, moving up the serving table as she dished out more vegetables for her and Henry. By now he was wearing a pout the size of Texas, and I knew for a fact a tantrum was brewing.

As soon as Mom had her back to me, I slipped out of the food tent. All I wanted to do was find a faraway trash can, dump the cukes, and then look for Margaret.

I'd taken three giant strides when Mom's voice rang out. "Lindy. Wait up, please. Henry needs a balloon hat."

I rolled my eyes, but not so she could see me. I felt like pointing out that (A) Henry didn't *need* a balloon hat—he'd already popped two of them earlier, before the parade—and (B) I didn't really have time to look for balloon hats, that I was supposed to be hanging out with Margaret, not my brother. But then I thought about band camp and bit my tongue.

"Come on," I said, motioning for Henry to follow me. He tore away from Mom, a huge smile stretched across his face.

"Bring Henry to the picnic tables by the courthouse. Your dad and I will be sitting with Evelyn,"

Mom said. She nodded at my plate. "And I expect you to show up with *all* those vegetables intact."

Well, I was doomed. There's no way I could even dump half of that mess down the trash, because Henry happens to be the world's biggest tattletale. I took off in a huff, wishing I could stuff every one of those cucumbers down his throat.

"Slow down, Lindy," he whined. "I can't keep up with you." He hung on to my belt loop as we wove through mobs of walking, talking vegetables, looking for the balloon hat clown. We circled a group of red-hot chili peppers dancing to a calypso band, dodged a couple of asparagus stalks juggling knives, and then stopped to watch a corn-on-the-cob eating competition. One guy had already plowed through twenty-two ears.

"Hey, there he is!" Henry pointed to a pink-haired clown who was twisting giant cucumber balloons into different shapes. We waited in line, got a couple of hats—because Henry begged me to wear one, too—and then I scanned the crowd, searching for Margaret. I saw her at a picnic table on the far side of the courthouse lawn. Her strawberry blond curls were easy to spot.

Oh. Great. Just my luck. Margaret was sitting within twenty feet of my parents. And not only that, she was sharing her table with a boy.

Wait. Was that who I thought it was? I shaded my eyes to make sure I wasn't seeing things.

I wasn't, and my luck had just gone from bad to totally terrible.

Sure enough, it was Gus Kinnard, the annoying know-it-all nerd who'd sat behind me in fifth-grade band and squeaked his saxophone into my ears every ten seconds. He practically drove me crazy all year, always acting like he knew the answer to every single thing. And ever since the spring concert, when I'd played my flute in a trio with him on sax and Margaret on trumpet, he'd acted as though the three of us were big buddies or something. Jeez. How did Margaret get stuck sitting with him? I hoped he didn't think he was going to hang out with us all day.

"I'm going to show Dad my balloon hat," Henry said, taking off. I charged after him, toward Margaret's table, and I'm not sure what happened next. My hat might've been blocking my vision, or maybe I tripped on my flip-flops, but I didn't see the Bloomsberry Cucumber Festival Princess or her plateful of strawberry shortcake until after we'd knocked into each other and she'd started screaming bloody murder.

I hopped backward, watching a huge, gooey piece of shortcake dribble down the dress of my least favorite person in the world, Angel Grimstone.

Chapter 3
Angel with an Attitude

"Oh, my God!" Angel screeched. "You did that on purpose." Her cheeks puffed out like a blowfish's, and I seriously thought she was going to spit on me.

I wasn't exactly on Angel Grimstone's list of Top Ten Cool Kids to Know. Actually, I'm sure I topped her list of Really Pathetic Losers to Avoid. We both played flute in the Bloomsberry Elementary band, and Angel had been steaming mad ever since I'd won first chair in January. Talk about a bad sport; she told everyone the only reason she'd lost was that I'd done something to mess up her flute.

The Princess snatched a sparkly tiara from the

ground and checked out the damage to her dress. Tears streamed down her face, leaving a trail of blue mascara. Her two friends, Lisa and Caroline, gave me dirty looks.

"That was, like, so totally rude, Lindy," Caroline said. "You totally ruined Angel's dress."

"Stupid idiot," Angel said. She wiped a blue smudge off her cheek and glared at me.

I glared back at her. "Actually, *idiot*, you're the one who bumped into me."

"Did not." Angel tossed the rest of her shortcake at me and stomped to a nearby table. Lisa and Caroline followed. They hovered over her with napkins, scrubbing the strawberry glaze even deeper into her white dress.

I quick checked my new purple T-shirt for damage. It was covered with whipped cream and a few loose strawberries, which I popped in my mouth, but not the first bit of stewed cucumbers. I didn't know whether to be disappointed or relieved. Not that I wouldn't have loved to see every last bit of that mushroom paste on the ground, but there's no way my mom would've believed it was an accident.

"Oh, Lin-deee," Angel sang as I took off. "I know why you're in such a hurry. You can't wait to go sit by your new boyfriend, Mr. Sexy-phone player."

Boyfriend? My cheeks burned as Angel and her friends snickered behind my back. What made them think that Gus Kinnard, the saxophone-squeaking nerd, was my boyfriend?

I hurried away from their laughter, making a quick stop for pink lemonade before plopping on the chair next to Margaret. Whew. What a morning. I wiped the sweat off my sticky forehead. It wasn't even the hottest part of the day yet, but already I felt more cooked than one of Granny Goose's cucumbers.

"Cool hat," Gus said from across the table. "You got another one?"

Ignoring him, I turned to Margaret. "You're not even going to believe—"

"Guess what?" Margaret grabbed my arm. She was so breathless with excitement she didn't seem to notice the pile on my plate. "Gus is going to band camp, too, and he just got a letter in the mail. It says the camp instructors are going to pick the thirty top-performing kids to play in a special concert at the governor's mansion. Ohmigosh. You've got to talk your parents into letting you go, Lindy. What if we get chosen?"

For a split second I forgot about the lunch disaster. My mind spun forward like a time machine, whirling me into the future. I saw myself in Tallahassee on the governor's lawn, right after my perfect flute solo. Electricity pulsed through the audience. "Bravo!" they cheered, jumping to their feet. I bowed once . . . twice . . .

But then the goose honked, and I snapped back to reality. I glanced over at my parents' table, remembering their hushed conversation last night, right after Dad had taken the call from the roof repair guy.

"We're getting slammed with home maintenance

this summer," he'd told Mom. "The estimate for a new roof is a couple of thousand more than I anticipated."

"That's not to mention Henry's new glasses," Mom said. "And something's wrong with the computer. I hate to say it, but it looks like we'll have to nix the you-know-what."

Margaret nudged me, her face still beaming, and my heart sank like an anchor in quicksand. How come it was always *my* family that didn't have money for the big stuff, the fun stuff, like extra-long weekends at Disney World and this band camp trip? And what if Margaret—and even Gus, by some miraculous accident—got chosen for the governor's concert and went to Tallahassee without me?

"Eew." Margaret pointed to my plate, and I shoved the no-money thoughts from my mind. "Why'd you take such a big serving of that?" she said.

"I didn't take it. I got stuck with it, after you took off."

Gus leaned over for a closer look. "What is it?"

I kept ignoring him, hoping he'd get the message.

"You need to help me eat this," I said to Margaret. "And hurry, before my mom comes over here." I looked out the corner of my eye. Sure enough, there sat the Carrot, glancing my way. Henry was on Dad's lap, probably trying to get out of eating his own measly portion of vegetables. I groaned when Granny Goose joined them. She hooked Pickles up to her chair and waved at me.

"I can't," Margaret said. "I'm allergic. If I ate that, it would give me terrible hives. And then my parents would have to rush me to the hospital emergency room. And then I'd probably get put in insensitive care or something." She took a bite of her fried chicken.

"You mean *intensive* care," Gus said. "Not insensi—"

"Since when are you allergic to cucumbers?" I said to Margaret.

"That's cucumbers?" Gus doubled over, snorting into his hand. It sounded like he'd hawked up a hair ball or something. "No way. It looks more like pickled toads." Margaret laughed so hard she spit a piece of chicken across the table.

"Oh, very funny. You both crack me up." My throat tightened when I looked at the nightmare on my plate. "This is something Granny Goose made. My mom's forcing me to eat it."

"Granny Goose?" Gus said. "You mean the save-the-animals lady? Hey, I heard she's got a three-legged alligator that sleeps by her bed."

Margaret's blue eyes widened behind her glasses. "Really? She's so cool. I love how she rescues all those poor animals."

"She may be cool, but she's a terrible cook," I said.

"How do you know?" Margaret said. "Maybe it doesn't taste as bad as it looks. You haven't even tried it yet."

"No, but I've smelled it, and so have you." Of course Margaret could act all la-di-da, because she wasn't the one who'd gotten stuck with a pile of slug guts. "Besides," I said, "Granny Goose belongs to my mom's cooking club, and I heard some of the members talking about the awful stuff she makes."

"Actually," Gus said, "it doesn't look that bad. Slide it over here. I'll try some first."

Before I could answer, he'd already snagged a droopy cucumber from the side of my plate. He popped it in his mouth. His face puckered up like my great-grandma's when she's not wearing her teeth. "It's pretty tasty," he said through pursed lips. "Really."

I sighed. This wasn't looking good, but I had to get it over with. My mom kept glancing my way, and she'd even done some kind of pantomime thing with her hand going from her plate to her mouth that I knew meant, "Eat those cucumbers."

I jabbed a slice with the least amount of sauce and lifted it to my mouth. But my fork stopped in midair, because something on the plate caught my eye.

Something gold.

Something heart-shaped.

Something that definitely wasn't a cucumber.

Chapter 4
The First Whiff of Trouble

"Hey!" I said. "What's that floating in the cucumbers?"

All three of our heads dived forward at the same time, and Gus's forehead knocked into mine. "Ouch! Watch it," I said, rubbing my eyebrow.

"There's nothing floating in there," he said.

"Oh, yeah?" I pushed the heart-shaped object to the side of my plate. "What do you call that?"

"I'd call it a heart, but it isn't floating. It was buried."

I ignored him and started wiping sauce off the heart. It didn't take but a few swipes to see it was covered with sparkly deep-red stones.

I picked it up. "Gosh. This looks like solid gold."

Margaret grabbed my hand. "Quick! Drop it! Don't even breathe on it."

I flung the heart down, my breath shooting out in quick spurts. "Why? What's wrong?"

Margaret threw a napkin over it. "Just act normal. Don't let on like anything's out of the ordinary."

"Me act normal? You're the one who's acting weird. I just want to look at it." I reached for the napkin.

She pushed my hand away. "No. We can't let anybody see it. We can't . . . tell . . . a soul."

"Why not?"

"Because," she whispered, "Granny Goose will get thrown in jail."

"Yep. That's a fact," Gus said, as if he knew exactly what she was talking about.

"Jail? Why would Granny Goose get thrown in jail? She's not a criminal."

"Haven't you heard about the robbery?" Margaret said. "That's Mrs. Grimstone's gold locket. It got stolen from her house."

"For real? It belongs to Angel's mom?" I said.

Gus shook his head. "Nope. Her grandmother." He scooted his chair around the table and parked it an inch from mine. "I read it's embedded with rubies, probably worth twenty thousand bucks, at least. Let me see it." He reached in front of me for the napkin.

I knocked his hand aside, then checked to make sure my mom wasn't watching before uncovering the locket myself. It sure did look like rubies, expensive ones, too. But then what did I know? The fanciest jewelry my mom owned was a shell necklace I made for her way back in kindergarten.

"Wait a minute," I said. "How do you know about any locket getting stolen from the Grimstones?"

"It was in the paper this morning," Margaret said.

"But this might not be the same locket. Maybe this is a piece of Granny Goose's costume jewelry that fell in the cucumbers while she was cooking. Or maybe it came off her goose's collar or something."

"Yep. That's it all right," Gus said. "There was a picture of it on the front page of the paper. Man, what're the odds of this happening—like one percent, maybe?"

Something clicked in my brain, and I thought back to breakfast, when Mom had handed my dad the newspaper and said, "Look at that. Right here in Bloomsberry. I hope they find the thieves."

I hadn't heard the rest of their conversation, because Henry had chosen that very minute to snatch my flute and run outside.

"Actually"—Gus went on—"a bunch of stuff got stolen from the Grimstones—all kinds of diamond jewelry, some rare coins. Pitayas, too. Six of them."

"What are Pitayas?" I said.

"Jeweled eggs," Gus said. "They're named after the

Russian guy who designed them, and they're made out of gold and emeralds. Mrs. Grimstone owned the whole collection."

"My mom said there's a huge reward out for the heirlooms," Margaret said.

My fingers curled around the locket. I licked my lips, barely able to utter my next words. "How much?"

"Five thousand dollars," Gus said.

"Oh, wow!" I sprang from my seat. "Come on. Let's find Officer Moore. I saw him earlier in a broccoli costume."

Margaret grabbed my hand. "Wait. What're you doing?"

"Hel-lo-o . . . What do you think I'm doing? I'm going to give this to the cops and collect the reward. We'll each get twenty-five hundred dollars. That means I'll be able to go to band camp."

"No, you're wrong," Gus said. His eyes narrowed into minicalculators. Click, click, click. "One thousand, six hundred, sixty-six dollars, and sixty-six cents, with two cents left over. That's what we'd each get."

I couldn't believe this kid. First he'd butted in on our lunch, and now he wanted to snag my reward money. I mean, it was me who nearly ate the locket. Did he actually think I'd split the money three ways? Well, I had news for Gus Kinnard—he wasn't getting a penny. I turned to leave.

"But it doesn't really matter. We won't get the reward anyway," he said.

"Why not?" I narrowed my eyes at Mr. Know-It-All.

"Because that locket is just one piece out of a dozen or so. And it's not even the most valuable. Some of the other things, like the eggs, are worth at least five times more."

"So what?" I said, but I could feel my happiness bubble deflating, like a bike tire with a slow leak.

"Think about it," he said. "Why would Mrs. Grimstone pay the whole reward for the least valuable piece? We wouldn't get more than a hundred dollars, tops. Thirty-three apiece after we split it up."

"Sit down, pleeease, Lindy," Margaret said. "Gus is right. Besides, we can't turn that locket in yet, anyway."

"Well, we can't keep it. We'll get in big trouble if we don't give it to the cops."

"I don't want us to *keep* it," Margaret whispered. "But if we turn it in right this minute, the police will ask where you found it. And then they'll think Granny Goose stole it, because you found it in her dish of cucumbers. And then she'll go to jail. For certain. Maybe for life."

Gus stuffed a handful of cherries in his mouth before saying, "Maybe noth lifth, but sheel get at leaf tin yearths, wiff time offth for good beha-for." He spit the seeds toward the ground, and—*oh, jeez!*—a couple of them ended up on my lap.

"Thorry," he said, picking at some gunk behind his lip.

Talk about annoying. I flicked the seeds back at him and dragged my chair all the way around to the other side of the table, so I was facing both of them.

"Granny Goose isn't a thief," I said to Margaret as I sat back down. I mean, how could anyone believe something that ridiculous? In fact, Granny Goose was probably the most kindhearted person in the whole state of Florida. I'd known about her animal rescue since I was a little kid, when she'd helped save the two abandoned kittens Margaret and I dug out of a Dumpster. They both were skinny from worms and covered with fleas. But thanks to Granny Goose, who nursed them back to health, they'd grown up to be fat, fluffy cats. I'd kept Pixie, and Margaret had Trixie. And Granny Goose had done it all for free, too.

"Nope. I won't take a cent," she'd insisted when my dad had tried to pay her. "I'm just happy to help these little critters out."

Mom said that after her husband died, Granny

Goose had carried on his business of animal rescue—
he'd been a veterinarian—except she refused to charge
people.

I scratched my head, totally puzzled. "This doesn't
make any sense. How could the locket have wound
up in her cucumbers?"

"The evidence points to her being the perpetrator," Gus said, "but I'll give it ninety-nine to one she's
being framed." He reached across the table and helped
himself to a huge swig of my pink lemonade.

I scowled at him, snatching my glass before he
could finish off the ice.

As I wiped the last bit of cucumber off the locket,
I thought about what we should do. My parents would
say to turn it in, even if it meant we didn't get any
reward. But then there was Granny Goose to think
about. Suppose she got put in jail for something she
didn't do? As much as I hated to admit it, Gus was
right. The evidence pointed to her.

"What if I just said I found the locket on the

ground?" I suggested. "Then the cops wouldn't suspect Granny Goose."

"Well, sure, that could probably work," Gus said. "But I know how we can keep her out of jail *and* earn the whole five thousand dollars—no sweat." He plopped his elbows on the table and rested his chin in his hands, staring at me. "Wanna know how?"

I ignored the WARNING: TROUBLE AHEAD sign flashing in the back of my mind. Instead, all I could think about was the money: 1,666 crisp one-dollar bills, stacked on my dresser. It would be all mine, and it would more than pay for band camp. My heart did a little swing dance as I pictured myself at the governor's mansion with a brand-new flute and a wad of cash in my backpack.

I sat straight up and looked Gus Kinnard in the eye. Because for once in his life, he might say something I actually wanted to hear.

"Yeah," I said. "How?"

Chapter 5
Gus Kinnard Is *NOT* My Boyfriend

"It's simple," Gus said. He wiped a glop of mashed potato from his chin, missing half of it. "All we have to do is find the real perp before the cops do."

Perp? As in perpetrator of a million-dollar heist?

Did Gus actually believe the three of us could hunt down a mastermind criminal all by ourselves? His idea was way crazy. Too crazy—I knew that. But I wanted that reward money, and I couldn't stop the *boing, boing, boing* of my heartbeat.

Margaret gasped. "You really think we can prove Granny Goose didn't steal the locket?"

"How?" I whispered, as if the deal were sealed

and we were all of a sudden conspirators. "We're not exactly detectives, you know. It would take forever."

"Nuh-uh," Gus said. "There can't be that many suspects. The newspaper said it looked like an inside job—maybe even someone who knows the Grimstones. Bloomsberry's a small town."

He tossed a cherry in the air and caught it in his mouth. "Granny Goose is innocent, and we can prove it. I'm really good at solving crimes. Actually, I just won an award for it."

"Oh, yeah?" I said, eyeing him suspiciously. "Like what award?"

"The NSCCB mystery of the month. I beat out more than thirty thousand participants."

"Oh . . . my . . . gosh." Margaret fell against the back of the chair, her eyes lit up like disco balls. "You won *that?* I can't believe it. What month?"

"May. So now there's a eight percent chance I'll win NSCCBer of the year."

I glanced from Gus to Margaret, then back at

Gus. It felt like I'd popped in on a meeting between a couple of cryptologists. "What the heck is NSPPB?"

"N-S-C-C-B," Gus said. "The Not-So-Clueless Crime Busters."

"It's the coolest online club ever," Margaret said, still looking dazed by his news. "I just found out about it last week. I really want to join, but my mom won't let me. She says I'm on the computer too much."

A tingly, nervous feeling fluttered around my stomach. Gus beat out thirty thousand participants in a crime-solving contest? Gosh, if that was the case, maybe he *could* find the heirloom thief—with Margaret's and my help, of course. It's not like the two of us were dumb bunnies. Besides, I didn't want Gus getting any big ideas about keeping more than his share of the reward money.

He folded his arms behind his head. "So. You guys want to go along with me or not?"

"I will if Lindy will," Margaret said.

I looked at the locket again, my heart thumping, and pictured the front page of the *Bloomsberry*

Sentinel: Local Youngsters Nab Heirloom Thief; Divvy Hefty Reward! Or even better: Talented Young Heroine on Her Way to Tallahassee; Hopes to Wow Governor with Flute Solo.

After overhearing my parents last night, I knew in my gut that winning the reward might be my only chance at band camp. I couldn't stand the thought of not going. The camp lasted two whole weeks, and practically everyone would be there, including Angel Grimstone. In fact, Angel hadn't stopped talking about camp ever since our teacher announced it. "I'm going to learn sixteenth notes and trills," she'd bragged. "I'm getting a new flute before I go, too. Grammy says I'll win first chair for sure next year."

Oooh—my blood boiled at the thought of it. I'd rather be appointed Granny Goose's recipe-tasting assistant than lose first chair to Angel Grimstone. And what if she got chosen for the governor's concert while I was home scrubbing toilets?

"Psst, Lindy." Margaret rapped the table.

"Are you going to help find the thief or not?"

I'd just opened my mouth to say, "You bet," when a giant stalk of broccoli approached us.

Uh-oh. It was Officer Moore. I grabbed the locket and held it to my side, flicking its tiny clasp. If he saw it, everything would be ruined. He circled our table— real slow—all the way around, stopping next to me. He leaned down to fiddle with the cuff of his costume.

He nodded at me and smiled. I smiled back, trying to look nonchalant, as if it were just another average day in my boring life. He got up, tipped his flowered green hat at us, and left.

I sank back in my chair, still flicking the locket's clasp. It opened. I glanced down, and staring back up at me was the Princess Grimstone. Right there in the palm of my hand, smiling like a hyena and holding a flute to her mouth.

"Aaack!" I tossed the locket on the table.

Margaret picked it up, then clutched her neck and squealed, "Eew! It's Angel."

"Let me see," Gus said.

But right as Margaret started to hand it to him, one side of her face scrunched up like she had a gnat in her eye. She made some kind of weird hissing noise and winked at me about ten times. "Hide it!" she said, flinging the locket back across the table.

"What's wrong?" My heart started racing again. Was someone watching us?

The only person I saw nearby was a farmer-looking guy in overalls and a straw hat, the same guy Granny Goose had nearly run into earlier, right before she'd dished out her cucumbers to me. He trudged by our table slower than a snail, but he was staring at the newspaper in his hand and didn't seem to be paying any attention to us.

Something shuffled in the grass behind me, like footsteps.

"Hurry *up*," Margaret whispered.

Next I heard giggles. Princess giggles.

"Oh, Lindeeee. Are you two going steady yet?"

More giggles. The Princess had her friends with her.

"Lindy and Gus, sitting in a tree, K-I-S-S-I-N-G."

"Oh, look, Lindeeee. Gus is sitting next to Margaret. Aren't you jealous?"

A shower of giggle spit sprayed my neck.

What I wanted to do was grab Angel's nose and twist it into macaroni. But my parents were too close by; they'd see the fight for sure. So I snatched the locket before Angel saw it and stuffed it in my pocket. I watched her from the corner of my eye. She and her friends were doubled over, laughing their heads off and pointing at my supposed boyfriend. Margaret glared across the table at them. Not Gus, though. He sat stiff in his chair, staring straight ahead without even blinking. Nothing moved except his jaw; it kind of twitched. His brown cowlick stuck straight up, like he'd just been electrocuted.

I knew I should say something. But what? If I stood up for Gus, it might look like he really was my boyfriend. So I got up, accidentally ramming my chair into the Princess, and went after another pink lemonade. I bought Gus one, too.

Luckily, Angel and her friends were gone when I got back. Unluckily, the Cucumber and the Carrot, followed by the Goose, were making a beeline for our table. My stomach went all woozy again, and this time it wasn't because of the secret in my pocket.

Sure enough, Mom took one look at my full plate and said, "Lindy, haven't you tried Mrs. Unger's dish yet?"

"Uh . . ."

The expression on Mom's face said, "Young lady, you'd better display the good manners I've crammed down your throat for the last eleven years, or else." What came out of her mouth was a cheerful "Go ahead and try a bite, dear. Mrs. Unger wants some feedback on whether she should revise her recipe."

Granny Goose stood by my side, watching . . . waiting . . . grinning.

Chapter 6

The French Connection

I couldn't stall any longer, because Mom's smile was getting thinner by the second. My chances of going to camp would get even worse if I made a scene. I jabbed a tiny piece of cucumber and ever so slowly guided it into my mouth. I gave it three good chews.

Oh, grossness.

I fought back a gag as the mushroom-flavored sludge coated my tongue. When I tried to swallow, it clung to the back of my throat like one of those sticky snot balls you get with a bad cold.

Granny Goose wrapped an arm around my shoulders. "Okay, honey. What's the verdict?"

"Um . . . eh . . ." I didn't dare tell her the truth; I'd never be allowed out in public again. "It's very unusual-tasting and . . . um . . . yes. It's perfect for the cook-off contest." I washed down my lie with two huge swigs of lemonade.

Granny Goose hooted. "God love you, Ann," she said to my mom, who of course was beaming by now. "What a doll of a daughter you've raised here. I'll tell you what. Now that I've got the green light from both of you and the Tarts, I'm good to go. I'm not so sure I need Chef François' sauce-making class after all."

Mom looked surprised. "Sauce-making class? I didn't realize you were considering—"

"*Bonjour! Bonjour*, my wonderful Tarts." A dark-haired man in a chef's hat and an apron flapped his arms at us from the courthouse steps. He blew a kiss our way, then shot across the lawn as if the seat of his pants was on fire. When he got to our table, he swept around me, Margaret, and Gus and went straight for Granny Goose. He stopped in front of her, grinning like a fox, twirling the tips of his sleek black mustache.

"*Madame*," the chef said, taking Granny Goose's hand. He puckered his lips and planted a noisy kiss on her knuckles, then turned to my mom and did the exact same thing. I wanted to barf on the spot, but Mom smiled politely at him, and Granny Goose giggled like a little kid.

"Aha!" François said. "The Carrot and the Cucumber—my two favorite Tarts, to be sure. You cannot hide your beauty behind these costumes. I would recognize you anywhere."

He smiled again, flashing a mouthful of teeth that were whiter than my mom's sheets after soaking in bleach for an hour. "Aaah," he said, "such a wonderful time we shared at the marvelous Mrs. Grimstone's this Tuesday, when I presented my soufflé demonstration for the Bloomsberry Tarts.

"And to you, *madame*," he said to Granny Goose, "*merci! Merci!* Accept, please, my heartfelt gratitude for distributing those many fliers regarding tomorrow's vegetable-carving extravaganza. I am forever indebted. How can I repay you?"

"No need for it," Granny Goose said, shaking her head. "I was happy to help."

François wagged his finger at her. "*Madame*, I am adamant. I must return the favor."

"Well, if you insist, you can give me a report on the stewed cucumbers. Sorry I couldn't let you taste them this morning. I had to let that sauce set," she said.

"Aha! I am already one footprint ahead of you, Mrs. Unger. I have just come from sampling your masterpiece. Magnificent!"

"Why, thank you, François," Granny Goose said. "I'm glad you like—"

"However, I regret to inform you the dish is not magnificent enough to win this cook-off you spoke of."

Granny Goose's face fell. "Well, darn. I'm sorry to hear that, but I guess you're the expert. I might have to rethink my entry."

"No, no, *ma chère*. That is not necessary. Your

cucumbers simply need to be stewed in a less pungent sauce. And that is why I am here. I implore you, madame, to immediately enroll in my sauce class, so that you can achieve the flair, the creativity, to win this upcoming contest."

"Well, heavens to Betsy," Granny Goose said after another fit of giggling. "I'm sorry to break it to you, François, but I'm not sure I can."

"What's that? You're not sure, you say? But you must." He got down on one knee, ignoring her goose, which was strutting in circles around him, practically honking its head off. He took her hand again. His lips turned down, into a pout. "Otherwise, *ma chère*, it will hurt me gravely. Your refusal shall become the knife that is plunged into this chef's soufflé. Poof! My heart will deflate in sorrow."

"Goodness gracious," Granny Goose said. By now her cheeks were so pink she looked like a cucumber with a fever. "I certainly don't want to disappoint you. And Lord knows I've just got to win that cook-off. Tell you what, I'll think it over."

"Please, but yes, do that," François said. "And beseech your fellow Tarts"—he winked at my mom—"to join you, *ma chère*. I will make room for them. I pledge that to you with sincere devotion." He pulled off his chef's hat and bowed. And then, with a flurry of good-byes and air kisses, he spun away to join another group of Tarts.

"Heavens." Mom fanned herself with a napkin. "What a charmer. He's certainly after you about that class, huh?"

"Yep. I'm tempted to follow him up on it, too. I know he's expensive, but the prize for that contest is twenty-five thousand dollars."

"That's quite a payoff," Mom said.

"Hot diggity, I'll say it is. And if I win, I'll put every cent of it to good use. I'm planning to expand the rescue service."

Mom put her hand to her chest, smiling and nodding

as Granny Goose explained how she and her friends wanted to set up a bigger network of animal caregivers. "We'll need supplies, sturdy pens . . . the whole she-bang. It's gonna take some bucks, that's for sure."

"What a wonderful idea, Evelyn. Count me and David in for a contribution. We're quite lucky to have such caring people like you in this community."

"Pshaw! I'm honored to do it; love every one of those animals, and we've got a boatload—gators, turtles, pelicans. You name it. Every type of injury, too. I'm telling you, Ann, it rips your heart out to see these magnificent creatures all smashed up and hurting, especially when it's us humans to blame."

Listening to Granny Goose, I felt a sudden, overpowering rush of admiration mixed with pangs of worry for her. There was no doubt in my mind. Besides my need for the reward money, I wanted to help her out of this jam, even if it meant working side by side with Gus Kinnard.

Chapter 7
The Scene at the Scene
of the Crime

As soon as Mom and Granny Goose took off across the courthouse lawn, Gus snapped his fingers. "Let's get started."

"Okay," I said. "But I want to hide this locket first. It's making me nervous."

"Let's take it to your garage, Lindy," Margaret said. "It's so messy in there we'll find all kinds of places to put it."

She was right about that. The garage was my dad's territory, and he wasn't what you would call a neat freak. But my heart still skipped a couple of beats because when I thought about it, hiding evidence seemed like risky business. "What if we can't solve this in a few days? You guys will have to go with me to turn the locket back in. Promise?"

"I promise," Margaret said.

Gus's face turned solemn. "Sherlock's honor. We'll claim we found it on the festival grounds, just like you said before, and then we realized later it was a missing heirloom. Technically, that's sort of the truth."

"Okay," I said, relieved to have that settled. "So after we hide it, then what?"

"Then we start investigating, figure out who framed Granny Goose," Gus said.

"It might be someone with a grudge against her," I said. "Someone who doesn't like her rescue service."

Gus shook his head. "Nah. Grudge crimes involving high-ticket thefts are rare—probably ten percent, tops. The motive is greed. The perp framed Granny Goose to take the heat off himself. He dropped the locket in the cukes, hoping whoever found it would make a big scene, turn it over to the cops. Then *voilà!* Granny Goose takes the rap, and the real thief is off the hook."

Margaret scowled, plopping her hands on her hips. "One thing's for sure, whoever did this is a totally heartless person."

"Well, they are *now* anyway." I pulled the locket from my pocket and grinned, then waved it in front of Margaret, waiting for her to laugh at my joke like she'd been laughing at every little thing Gus said. But she didn't even crack a smile.

"We'll need to get over to Granny Goose's house soon, check things out, ask her some questions," Gus said. "But first, we should start at the scene of the crime. We'll have a ninety-eight percent chance of getting critical info there."

"Wow," Margaret said. "How do you know all this stuff?"

"NSCCB. It's all about checking facts, calculating odds. That's how I solved the May mystery."

During the whole walk to my house Gus went on and on about NSCCB—yap, yap, yap about crime statistics and club guidelines and how he figured out this and that to win the contest. Margaret lapped every word of it up like she was spellbound, but by the time we opened my garage door, I was ready to cover my ears.

We wandered around for a couple of minutes, looking for the perfect hiding spot. Gus said we should definitely put it up high, on the top shelf of Dad's tools. "Odds are ninety to one he won't find it up there."

Margaret agreed with him, of course, because she still couldn't get over how he'd won crime buster of the month.

"No. That's not the best place," I said. Gus may have been a contest winner, but I knew my dad. I stuck the locket, still wrapped in its napkin, behind a container of Grubb's grime remover. "It'll be lots safer back here." I felt superconfident about that, maybe 99 percent, because I'd never once in my life seen my dad clean grime off anything.

We were standing outside the garage, talking about what to do next, when I noticed the farmer-looking guy I'd seen at the festival. He still had the newspaper in his hand, but I didn't think he was reading it. In fact, I got an eerie feeling he'd been watching us. He crossed the street, climbed into a rusty green pickup truck, and took off.

I started to mention it, but Gus interrupted my train of thought. "You guys ready to hit the crime scene?"

"Sure." Margaret pulled a rubber band from her pocket and gathered her thick curls into a lopsided ponytail. "Let's go."

"Hang on a second," I said. "I've got to check in with my mom first." I found her upstairs changing out of her carrot costume.

She smiled when I asked if I could hang out with Gus and Margaret for the afternoon. "I'm tickled you two are warming up to him. You know, I saw his dad at the last PTA meeting, and he mentioned how lonely Gus has been since Antoinette's death. Jack's worried about him, says he doesn't seem to have any friends and that kids tease him because he's a bit of an egghead."

Well, she had that right—the egghead part, anyway.

Mom checked her watch. "Remember to be home by three-thirty, and not a minute later. We've got a busy afternoon lined up. And remind me next year not to cochair this festival."

I waved good-bye and bounded down the steps— two at a time—and that's when I started feeling kind of bad about Gus. No wonder he was lonely. His mom had died in a car crash just last July, his only brother was away at college, and I'd heard Mom say his dad worked all the time. I made a silent vow to be nicer to Gus Kinnard.

About ten minutes later my vow got seriously tested.

"Wait a minute," I said when Gus slipped through an open gate into Palmetto Estates, where the Grimstones lived. I read the sign over his head: WELCOME TO PALMETTO ESTATES: LUXURY LIVING AT ITS MOST EXQUISITE. WARNING! GATED COMMUNITY. RESIDENTS AND GUESTS ONLY. AREA PATROLLED BY SECURITY GUARDS. VIOLATORS PROSECUTED.

"Shouldn't we find another way in or something?" I pointed to the surveillance camera.

Margaret chewed at a cuticle, looking around nervously. "Do you think someone's watching us, you know, like from a guard tower?"

"Nah," Gus said. "Don't sweat it. My dad comes out here all the time to see the Grimstones; he's their attorney. He says that fifty percent of the time there's no guard on duty."

After five more minutes of walking, Gus finally stopped us across the street from the Grimstones'. He pointed at the bright green hedge surrounding their front yard. It'd been clipped, shaved, buzzed, and styled into different sea creatures. "Cool, huh?" he said. "My dad says some famous artist from Miami does their shrubbery. He says they have the biggest flower garden he's ever seen in their backyard, too."

We crossed the street to the Grimstones' property, then poked our heads between a bushy dolphin and a giant sea horse. Their house was huge, more like a mansion. A pebbled pathway lined with palm trees, flowering bushes, and mermaid fountains wound through the yard and up to a wraparound porch.

"The *Sentinel* said there wasn't any sign of forced entry. That's why the cops think the thief must be someone they know," Gus said.

The front door opened. Margaret gasped. She dropped to the sidewalk, snagging her glasses on the sea horse. They bounced off my toe and landed under the dolphin. She dived after them, falling facedown on the concrete.

A shrill voice rang out from the door. "That is *exactly* what I told Howard. I said, 'I will *not* hesitate to call the police at the first whiff of intruders around here, even if they are nothing more than children.'"

Chapter 8
Sly like Spies

I didn't move a muscle. Gus stood next to me, frozen solid as a Popsicle. Margaret stayed sprawled on her stomach on the sidewalk. You would've thought she was dead, except her hand crept across the concrete and fumbled under the dolphin for her glasses.

A second person appeared on the porch. I stared at her for a second before recognizing the white-blond hair gelled into spikes, the leopard tank top and stretch pants, and the floppy leopard bag hanging off her shoulder. "Hey," I whispered, "that's Cricket from Shear Magic. What's she doing here?"

Cricket headed down the porch steps and around

a pebbled path toward the driveway. "You know, Mrs. Grimstone," she called over her shoulder, "if I were you, I'd have security out here patrolling twenty-four seven."

"Believe me," Mrs. Grimstone said from the porch, "I am considering it. And thank you again for returning my neck scarf, Cricket." She patted her puffy auburn curls. "Now, about my hair . . . I'm not wild over that tint you used Tuesday. There's still some irritation behind my ears, and I think the color should be deepened. I'm going to have you redo it tomorrow after my pedicure."

"Uh . . . sure. I'll see what I can do." Cricket closed the door to her car and flicked an index finger in a quick wave to Mrs. Grimstone. "Take it easy."

"That's precisely what I intend to do. Howard and I are staying in for the day. No Tart activities for me, I'm afraid. I'm anxious to get a progress report from the police." The front door closed behind her.

Cricket revved her motor a couple of times before backing out of the driveway.

I dodged around the corner of the hedge, pulling Margaret with me. We watched the car roll down the street.

"Hey," Gus said. He'd wedged himself behind some bushes that ran alongside the Grimstones' house and was pointing at a screened porch in the back. "That's Mr. and Mrs. Grimstone. Let's crawl back there. We might hear some details about the robbery."

One by one, an army of goose bumps marched up my arms. My mom's face flashed before my eyes: the same face she wore every time she nagged: "If I've said it once, I've said it a hundred times. You must not act on impulse. Just because your friends try something, that doesn't mean you should . . ." Blah, blah, blah.

But this was a special circumstance.

I checked out the thick, flowering bushes. No one could possibly see us in there. And it wasn't as though we were doing anything really wrong, or bad.

The way I saw it, we were the good guys. So what was the harm?

I dropped to the ground. Margaret followed, even though she looked more scared than I'd ever seen her. We clawed our way through the thick, scratchy bushes, batting mosquitoes and no-see-ums from our faces. Once we were within a couple of feet of the porch, Gus put his finger to his lips. The sound of ice clinking in glasses and muffled voices floated out through the screen.

I cocked my head, straining to hear the conversation.

"That's exactly what I'm trying to tell you, Howard. If you would let me complete a sentence without interrupting—thank you very much—you might understand what I'm talking about."

"Sorry. Go ahead," a man mumbled.

"I'm sorry, too, dear. I didn't mean to snap; it's just that I'm so terribly distraught over this. What I was saying is, the detective instructed me to think things over, to recall anything out of the ordinary."

Mumble, mumble.

Mrs. Grimstone continued. "You remember, don't you, that the Bloomsberry Tarts were here two days ago for François Pouppière's presentation."

"Who's Francine Poop-hair?"

"Poo-pee-air! Fran-swa Pouppière. For heaven's sake, Howard, I've already told you—François owns Simply Paris, that quaint little restaurant downtown. He was gracious enough to give a demonstration on soufflés this Tuesday right here in our kitchen. If you weren't always out of town on business, you'd remember these details."

Then came sniffles and Mr. Grimstone again. "There, there," he said. "I understand your anxiety over this."

"Thank you, Howard. Now as I was saying . . ." Mrs. Grimstone continued, her voice fading in and out. I didn't have a clear view of her, but I could tell she was pacing the porch. "To my knowledge, only one of the Tarts left the kitchen. She was gone for several minutes, certainly enough time to enter our upstairs study. Oh! If only I hadn't laid those pieces out to be appraised. I'm absolutely sick."

My cheeks tingled with excitement. I couldn't believe our luck. We were actually listening to the inside scoop about the heist, straight from Mrs. Grimstone's mouth. If we could only get a suspect's name, a description even.

"She followed François around like a puppy, asking him the most ludicrous questions about mushroom paste."

Mushroom paste? My ears perked up, like antennae. Margaret nudged me, a worried look on her face.

"Oh. You mean . . ." Another mumble from Mr. Grimstone.

"No, Howard. I am talking about that character who lives across the pond. It's her goose that's been wreaking havoc in this yard. I've got a hunch she's our thief, and I am most certainly calling the—"

Margaret clutched my arm.

"Did she just say what I thought she did?" I whispered. "That she's going to call—"

"The cops!" Margaret squealed. "She's going to call the cops on Granny Goose. Ohmigosh. What should we do?"

"We got some good info here, just like I thought," Gus said. "Let's head over to Granny Goose's, see if she's home. We've got to piece some things together."

We shot back through the bushes until we'd reached the front corner of the house. We were just getting ready to crawl into the sunlight when an odd-sounding honk stopped us.

Pickles!

She honked again and sped across the lawn, straight for us. She dropped a worn duct-taped wallet from her bill, then wriggled between the branches and squatted on my lap. Not a second later a muddy work boot landed on the wallet, inches from my knee.

"Where the heck's that duck?" a man grumbled. "I'm gonna get rid of that pest if it's the last thing I do."

I clamped my teeth and held tight to Pickles, praying she wouldn't give us away. I poked a couple of branches aside and peered up through the white flowers.

My heart flipped like a pancake when I saw the straw hat, rumpled overalls and dirty T-shirt. I recognized this guy, all right: the farmer-looking man from the festival. The same guy who'd walked by the garage while we were hiding the locket.

A burly hand yanked the leaves back. "Okay, miss," the man said. He stared straight at me. "Hand it over."

Chapter 9
A Grim Encounter

The man's hawk eyes blazed in the sunlight. "You heard me. Give it here," he grumbled.

The locket! Had he seen me with it?

"Uh . . . I, uh . . . don't . . ." My mouth went dry.

"I said to give that ver-mit here."

"What ver-mit?" I squeaked.

"The bird. It's got my wallet."

"Oh. You mean Pickles." I handed the goose to Margaret and pushed myself up through the flowers. "Um . . . excuse me, sir, but Pickles doesn't have your wallet."

"Heck he don't. Just took off with it. I saw it myself."

"Uh, sir. You're standing on your wallet."

He snatched it off the ground, glaring at me the whole time. "I still want the duck."

"Actually," Gus said, hopping up beside me, "it's a goose, not a duck. And we've been looking all over for her. We're here to take her home."

"Nuh-uh. That bird ain't goin' nowhere except the pound. Been out here doin' its business in my gardenias, and I ain't gonna stand for it." He reached for Pickles, but she pecked at him.

He drew his hand back. "Forget the pound. I'm gonna fry that darn thing up for supper."

"Oh, no!" Margaret jumped up. "You can't cook this goose. She's innocent. We'll take her home, we promise." She squeezed Pickles against her chest, causing another honk, and this time it was louder than a car horn.

"What's the racket out there?"

I whipped my head around. We were standing several feet from the porch, but I could still see

Mrs. Grimstone's nose flattened against the screen. "What is it you've got there, Leonard?" she yelled. "That wretched goose again?"

"Worse than that, Mrs. Grimstone. You've got trespassers."

"Trespassers? Hold on to them, for God's sake. We'll be right there."

I gulped. Sweat poured from my forehead, my armpits, my neck. Even my ears. What if this Leonard guy knew about the locket? What if he said something to Mrs. Grimstone?

Five seconds later she rounded the back corner of her house. She charged across the lawn on her high-heeled sandals, stopping in front of me. A chubby man with sweaty pink skin and damp circles under each armpit panted after her. He fanned himself with an unlit cigar.

Mrs. Grimstone stood with her hands on her hips, staring at us like we were blobs of swamp scum. "Well, well. What have we here?"

"Say they're after the goose, ma'am," Leonard said.

"That's right," I said, my knees quivering. "We'll take her right home."

"And why should we relinquish this goose to you?" Mrs. Grimstone said. "We've had a continuous problem with it, and I'm ready to turn it over to animal control. Call security, Howard."

"Now, Hazel, calm down for a minute," Mr. Grimstone said. He took a couple of steps back, chewing on his cigar as he looked us over. "We've got enough to deal with here. Why not let these youngsters take it home? They look like responsible kids."

"Oh, we are," I said.

"Really and truly," Margaret said. "We'll get Pickles off your hands right away."

Gus checked his watch. "Actually, we're running late. We'd better get going. Nice to meet you, everyone."

Mr. Grimstone pulled the cigar out of his mouth. "Likewise. And take care of that goose."

As we edged toward the sidewalk, Mrs. Grimstone said, "I want you children to remember this is a gated community. In the future, I'd appreciate your not romping through here without an invitation. Oh, and Leonard, will you run to the nursery for some colorful annuals to place around my three-tiered fountain, please? It's looking bare."

"Yes, ma'am."

"One more thing," she said, as he jingled the keys in his pocket. "I'll need you to get an earlier start this Monday. These gardenias should be pruned. They're an absolute sight."

"I'll be here," he said, but he looked about as happy as someone who just got told he had five whopper cavities. He glanced at me again, and something about that look, like we were in on the same secret, nearly fried the freckles off my face.

Chapter 10
Just the Facts, Please

A rusty green truck rattled by us on our way out of Palmetto Estates. Leonard was driving. Pickles bobbed her head frantically, honking at him from Margaret's arms.

"Shhh," Margaret said, stroking Pickles's ruffled feathers. "If you don't watch out, he'll cook you for dinner."

I nodded, not doubting that possibility at all. I'd been thinking about Leonard since we'd left the Grimstones, and I had a couple of suspicions. "That guy was at the Tarts' table before Granny Goose dished out the cucumbers," I told Margaret.

"You're right. I remember his straw hat."

"And then he came by our table when I had the locket out. He even walked by my house right after we hid it. I saw him."

"Could've been a tail," Gus muttered, as if he were thinking aloud. "Twenty percent odds, maybe."

"It's like he was following us, like he knew I had the locket," I said.

"Ohmigosh," Margaret said breathlessly. "He even works for the Grimstones. Maybe he's the one trying to frame Gran—"

"Yep. A definite possibility," Gus muttered again. "Seventy-five percent of all property thefts are perpetrated by someone close to the victim."

"So you agree?" I said to Margaret. "You think Leonard's the—"

"Nope," Gus said. "Too soon to make assumptions. We don't have enough on him. What we need are cold, hard facts." He held up one finger. "Guideline number one, NSCCB: 'Never jump to conclusions. Stick to the facts.'"

Margaret nodded. "I read that on the Web site."

"You want facts," I said, about a hair more than irritated with Gus. "I'll give you facts. One, Leonard's poor. He drives a ratty old truck and holds his wallet together with duct tape. Two, he doesn't like Mrs. Grimstone very much. Three, since Leonard works for the Grimstones, he must've known all about the heirlooms. I bet he even has a key to their house."

"Those aren't facts," Gus said. "Those are motives."

We kept walking as we argued over facts and motives and what Gus called circumstantial evidence—"it plays a key role in about forty percent of solved crimes," he said—and by the time we made it out of Palmetto Estates, I grudgingly realized he was right. We still needed more information about Leonard before declaring him the thief.

Gus's plan was to scope out Granny Goose's and get details of everything that'd happened early that morning, without tipping her off about what we were up to. "Remember, mum's the word. That's guideline number six of—"

"NSCCB," Margaret said along with him. She jabbed his side and laughed.

When we got to Granny Goose's, Margaret ran up the porch steps and rang the doorbell. No answer. She rang again. Still nothing.

Gus took off to check the backyard while I peered through the porch window, looking for any signs of activity. I thought I heard a duck quacking inside, but I couldn't see past the birdcages in the window. I ran out to the front yard and looked down the street again.

"Nothing out back but a bunch of animals," Gus yelled from the side of the house.

"They've already arrested her. That's why she's not here," Margaret announced. She stood white-faced at the top of the porch steps, holding Pickles. "Do you realize this poor little goose could be homeless? She could die of starvation."

Her eyes misted up, and then she planted a noisy

kiss on Pickles's bill. One thing I knew for sure: if Granny Goose really had been arrested, Pickles would end up in a crib beside Margaret's bed. She'd probably be waddling after us to school every day next fall, too, and sitting in the audience during our band concerts. No way would Margaret let her get taken to the pound, because next to Granny Goose, Margaret's got the softest heart of anyone I know. She can't even stand to see a dried-up worm on the sidewalk.

"Nah," Gus said. "She's probably still at the festival. Even if Mrs. Grimstone has called the cops, they couldn't have booked Granny Goose yet. They don't work that fast. What they'll do is take a statement from her, then get a search warrant if there's evidence or probable cause."

We decided to wait on the porch a while longer for Granny Goose, but after several minutes I remembered my mom's instructions. I asked Gus the time.

"A quarter to three. Why?"

"I've got to be home at three-thirty. I have to help my mom peel and chop cucumbers."

"For the cucumber smoothie booth?" Margaret asked.

"Yeah, I have to have them all done tonight."

"I can't believe you're getting stuck with that job," she said. "Your mom makes you do the craziest things."

"I know, and it's going to take me three whole hours, at least. Geesh. Whoever dreamed up the dumb idea of a cucumber smoothie booth anyway?" I sighed, dreading the thought of all the peeling and dicing that awaited me.

"Actually," Gus said, "my mom did. She made up the recipe a few years ago, when she was president of the Tarts' club. The booth makes a lot of money." His face flushed, and then he ducked behind the swing. He cupped his hands around his eyes and pressed his nose against Granny Goose's window.

I swallowed a gulp, wishing I could snap my fingers and magically suck my words back in. "Oh. Uh . . . sorry," I muttered. "I didn't know that."

Margaret nudged me, and I glanced over my shoulder again at Gus, feeling terrible.

I didn't know what was running through his mind, but I couldn't help wondering how it must feel to all of a sudden not have a mom in your life. No one fussing over the little details, like whether you'd flossed between *all* your teeth or if you had clean sheets and plenty of blankets on your bed or if every one of the twenty-five library books got returned on time.

I looked sideways at Margaret, and I could tell by the frozen frown on her face that she felt as bad as I did. It was as if a thick cloud had covered the porch, muffling everything but the soft thump of my heartbeat. Gus was still peering in the window, and I couldn't think of one thing to say to make him feel better. I sat perfectly still beside Margaret, wondering how long the uneasy silence would go on.

Finally I leaned over the back of the swing and said, "Uh, we only got one measly suspect here so far.

What do you think we should do next?"

"That's just what I was going to ask," Margaret said.

He turned to face us. Still feeling a little nervous, I gave him a weak smile. He grinned back, then Margaret smiled, and all of a sudden it was like the old Gus had kicked into action.

He circled the swing, and we'd just started reviewing our circumstantial evidence again when a familiar-looking cucumber called from the sidewalk.

Chapter 11
Who Framed Granny Goose?

"Well, hot diggity," Granny Goose said. "Look who's here. You must be back for seconds."

We rushed to the lawn to greet her and explain how we'd found Pickles at the Grimstones' house.

She scowled when we told her about Leonard. Wagging a finger in her goose's face, she said, "Shame on you. Can't I leave you alone for half an hour? And don't give me that sassy look, young lady. It's the second time today you've gotten that scallywag's bowels in an uproar. The next time you'll end up on his table with a fork in your rump."

I elbowed Margaret. "Uh, Mrs. Unger, did you say

this is the *second* time today Leonard saw Pickles? What happened the first time?"

"Same old, same old, honey. She got out and crossed the pond to their yard. He brought her back here in a huff. Claimed she was tearing up the flower garden."

"Was that this morning?" Gus said.

"Yep. Wanted to talk to me about plugging the hole in my fence. Says the Grimstones are fed up with Pickles getting loose. I didn't have time to hash it out with him, though. I was in a hurry. Had three dishes to get ready for the festival.

"Besides," she said, winking at us, "I'd rather wrestle a crocodile than make small talk with Leonard Snout."

"He's not very friendly, huh?" Margaret said.

"You've got that right, honey. He's had a bee up his boxers ever since he lost the family farm last year. Can't reason with him."

"He lost his farm?" I said. "How'd that happen?"

"Mismanagement, pure and simple. Couldn't pay the bills, so he went bankrupt. Anyway, the man's got a green thumb, so I guess that's why the Grimstones hired him as their flower gardener."

Good thing Granny Goose is a big talker, I thought, because we'd just learned another whopper of a motive for Leonard.

We followed her back up the porch steps to her locked front door. By now my brain was whirling faster than the spin cycle on Mom's washing machine. I felt sure Leonard was our man. He had motives, several of them. He'd been lurking around the Tarts' tent, maybe even spying on me. And he'd been at Granny Goose's this morning. I still had more questions regarding that bit of news, but I didn't want to tip her off about anything.

Granny Goose set her food dishes on the swing and peeked inside her mailbox. "Humph," she muttered. "Where the heck did I put those keys?" She lifted the doormat. Nothing there, so she had us check under every single flower pot on the porch.

"Well if that doesn't beat all." She dug through her shoulder bag, pulling out a checkbook, a wad of Kleenex, and a handful of papers.

"Look." Margaret pointed to a leaflet Granny Goose was holding. "Isn't that the chef?"

"That's him all right, honey. He brought a stack of these fliers over today, had me running all over the place, handing them out."

I read the bold print under a smiling photograph of François:

Voilà!

Who can sculpt roses from carrots?

Who can carve sailboats out of cucumbers?

It is me (yes, *c'est moi!*).

C'est François!

Come watch this renowned chef and esteemed vegetable sculptor create a masterpiece of gorgeous, edible art.

Friday, June 17. 1:00 P.M. at Simply Paris, downtown Bloomsberry.

Special festival price—only $35 per person.

I was still thinking of how I could ask more questions about Leonard, without sounding too nosy, when Gus spoke up. "Mrs. Unger, did François drop these fliers at your house *this morning*?"

I raised my eyebrows and looked at Margaret. François? Wait a minute, I remembered him and Granny Goose talking about fliers earlier. Maybe all the evidence didn't point to Leonard.

"What's that you said, honey?" Granny Goose's face was buried in the bag again.

"I was just curious," Gus said, raising his voice. "Since François is a chef and all, did he help you *prepare* any of your dishes this morning? Like, you know, maybe add an ingredient or two?"

She kept rooting through her bag, and when she finally answered, her voice sounded muffled. "Well, now that you ask, I wondered if he didn't add a touch of pepper to my beet salad when I was out back. There." She pulled out a key ring and grinned. "Found them."

Margaret's eyes sparkled with excitement. "You mean François was *alone* in your kitchen? *All by himself* with the cucum—"

"Hey! I've got an idea." Gus winked at me and Margaret behind Granny Goose's back and put his finger to his lips. "How about we find that hole in the fence and fix it for you, Mrs. Unger?"

"Now that's one heck of a plan. I like the way you think, kid. Go ahead and take Pickles with you; she'll lead you straight to it."

I cringed when she said, "And while you're at it, I'll get out of this costume and whip us up some snacks."

We'd just rounded the side of the house when Granny Goose called from the door. "I almost forgot, kids. Don't mess with any of the caged critters back there, especially Hogjaw. He's my snapper. Oh, and don't let Charlie worry you. His pen's certified by the Reptile Rescuers Association; he couldn't get out if his life depended on it."

I didn't even stop to think about who she meant by Charlie, because one giant question was stuck in my brain: Who'd framed Granny Goose, Leonard or François?

"Ohmigosh," Margaret said when the front door closed. "They both were here this morning. Now we've got two suspects."

"We've hit pay dirt," Gus said. "François was at the festival, too. He had a helping of her cukes. Maybe he was looking for something besides sauce flavor, know what I mean? If he was the one to find the locket and turn it in, then no one would suspect he stole it in the first place."

"He was at Mrs. Grimstone's on Tuesday for the soufflé demonstration, too," Margaret said.

"You know what?" I said to Gus. "I think we should split up and follow them both. Margaret and I can go after François. You take Leonard."

"Bad idea," Gus said. "Classic mistake. NSCCB, guideline three: One step at a time, Sherlock. Guideline nine: There's strength in numbers. We should stick together, scout around here first. Let's try to get more info out of Granny Goose, like who went where in her house this morning, and was anyone else in her kitchen? But remember, we can't let on to her what we're after. That could blow everything."

Margaret grinned, then ran her pinkie finger around her mouth. "My lips are sealed, Sherlock."

I stood behind them, rolling my eyes. It seemed like in the last couple of hours, Margaret had gone along with every single NSCCB thing Gus said. What would happen if she joined that online club? Would she start hanging around Gus all the time, spouting off statistics and guidelines like he did?

Gus unlatched the gate. "Keep your eyes peeled for anything out of the ordinary."

He pushed the gate open, and the very first thing I thought was that *everything* in Granny Goose's yard looked out of the ordinary. In fact, it felt like we'd just been airlifted into Wild Florida Safari. Her yard, which stretched all the way back to a fence that separated it from Palmetto Pond, was filled with a jumbled assortment of animal pens and coops and cages. They were scattered throughout orange trees, coconut palms, and giant oaks.

A chicken squawked a greeting, and a pile of tabby cats stared sleepily at us from a nearby lawn chair. They rolled away from each other like balls of fuzzy yarn, stretching and yawning. Then one by one they jumped off the chair and curled around our legs, meowing as they followed us. We hadn't gotten but a few steps farther before three ducks and a scruffy, limping pelican joined our parade.

We all traipsed after Pickles, winding our way around pens of skunks, rabbits, raccoons, opossums, a fox, and even a couple of snakes. The thick Florida air grew hotter and stickier by the second. I was seriously wishing for an icy cold drink when feathers rustled above us and something called, "Who cooks for you? Who-cooks-for-you-all?"

Margaret grabbed Gus's arm. "What's that?"

He pointed to the top of a giant oak tree. "Cool.

It's a barred owl. That's their call: 'who-cooks-for-you-all?'"

A huge pair of black eyes peered through clusters of Spanish moss. "Oooh," Margaret cooed. "It's so adorable. Look! See its little yellow beak? Hey, up there," she called. "Who cooks for you, too?"

The owl called again, even louder. Margaret giggled, then Gus called back at the owl, and then Margaret busted up laughing, and . . . well, let's face it, no way was I ever going to tear her attention away from that bird. Margaret had always been crazy for animals, ever since we were little kids, and it looked like Gus was, too. In fact, I wasn't sure either of them remembered our original plan, the one our Not-So-Clueless Crime Buster had just laid out: Check for clues; ask Granny Goose more questions.

I left them standing under the tree cavorting with the owl, while I followed the ducks, the pelican, the cats, and the goose through a maze of flowering bushes.

That's when I met Charlie.

Chapter 12

An *Eggstremely Eggciting* Discovery

I stood glued to my flip-flops, staring at a scaly three-legged alligator, sunning himself in a plastic wading pool. And then I must've yelped even louder than the barred owl, because Margaret and Gus, white-faced, came racing around the hibiscus plants. I stuck out my arm to stop them.

"What happened?" Gus said.

"G-Gator," I said, still gasping for breath. "There . . . in the pool. Don't get too close. You might wake him up."

Margaret's jaw dropped open. "You were right," she said to Gus. "Granny Goose really does have a three-legged alligator."

Gus scratched his head, blinking his eyes with astonishment. "Wow. I . . . uh . . . well, I kinda just made up that part about the three legs."

Margaret nudged him and chortled. "You must have ESP or something."

"Yeah," he said. "Maybe it runs in my family. My dad says his uncle had . . ." Yada, yada, yada. On he went, and then they started talking about what might've happened to the gator's leg, which led to a big zoology discussion about all the other injured wildlife in Granny Goose's backyard, which meant that no further evidence was being discovered. I reminded them why we were there, and they both said, oh, yes, they'd get busy and scope out the backyard.

That left me—all by myself, never mind it'd been Gus's big idea in the first place—to plug the opening in the fence. I did have company, though. Pickles and her friends paraded in circles around me as I stuffed rocks into the getaway hole.

"Well, that takes care of that," I said to Pickles

after shoving in the last rock. "Doesn't look like you'll be causing any more problems at the Grimstones' for a while."

I looked around for Gus and Margaret, wondering if they'd found anything that could link us to who'd framed Granny Goose, like footprints, torn pieces of clothing, store receipts—the kinds of things TV detectives always search for. I spotted them up by the animal pens. Gus was pointing to Charlie's pool, and both of them were laughing. It seemed as though they'd totally forgotten about our time crunch, because they sure weren't in any rush.

But then, why should they be?

They weren't the ones who desperately needed money for band camp. In fact, both of them had paid the fee weeks ago. As I watched them jabbering to the armadillo, I couldn't help feeling a twinge of jealousy. For the tiniest instant, I wished it were one of them—preferably Gus—whose family couldn't afford the band camp tuition.

I was still wiping the dirt and sand off my shorts when Granny Goose called from her deck. "Hey, kids, come on up for a bite to eat."

Gus and Margaret tore across the yard and up the steps as if they hadn't eaten in a couple of days. They didn't even check on me; it was like they'd forgotten I existed.

Well, fine by me. Let them get stuck with sweet-and-sour brussels sprouts or mushroom caps stuffed with hominy grits. I couldn't have cared less. I sat against the fence, petting the pelican and blending into the weeds, hoping Granny Goose would forget about me, too.

No such luck. When she called the second time, I groaned and headed toward her house.

I tromped across the yard and up the back steps, crossing my fingers that we could get some more information from her and praying she wouldn't serve the leftover cucumbers. When I paused at the top of the steps to wait for Pickles, I noticed an enclosure jutting out from under the deck, right below me. It was surrounded by wire fencing. The pen was filled with aloe plants, cacti, and a miniature pond. A speckled turtle the size of a small boulder snoozed on a log inside it. It must be the snapper Granny Goose had mentioned.

As I turned for the door, something else in the pen caught my attention. I raced back down the steps and peered through the wire.

Uh-oh.

Okay. I may not have been a zoologist like Margaret or Gus, but I was 100 percent sure of one thing: Snapping turtles don't lay golden eggs.

In fact, the egg in the pen looked suspiciously like the stolen ones Gus had described: miniature gold ovals, embedded with emeralds, made by some famous Russian guy named Pitaya.

I swallowed a gulp, checking over my shoulder. Coast clear, except for Pickles. She watched me curiously from the deck. I reached through the wire fence for the egg, but it was out of my grasp. The door to the pen was locked, and the fence was too high to climb over. I'd have to find a long stick, poke it through the wire, then nudge the egg out from under the log. Before I did that, though, I should check the turtle's pen carefully. Maybe there were other heirlooms in there.

Aha! I saw something. It lay partially hidden under the aloe plant. I reached through the wire fence again and picked it up. Definitely not an heirloom. It was a small metal medallion with "Ford" inscribed on both sides. An unclosed jump ring dangled from a hole in the medallion; it must've fallen off someone's key ring. I stuck it down in my pocket. "Collect all evidence, no matter how insignificant," I'd heard Gus tell Margaret. It was guideline number five of the NSCCB.

Now for the egg. I found a stick near the deck and poked it through the wire. I was sweating all over by now, prodding at the egg, trying to loosen it. I'd just managed to work the tip of my stick between the egg and the log, when . . .

"CHOW'S COMIN' UP!"

Chapter 1️3️

Ducks in Diapers, Etc.

I leaped a foot off the ground, almost high enough to clear the top of the turtle pen. Holy cow! How long had Granny Goose been standing on the deck? Had she seen the egg? I plastered my arms to my sides and turned to face her.

Her gray hair was tied back with a bandanna, and she'd changed out of her cucumber costume into cutoff jeans and a turquoise T-shirt with sharks on the front that said "I dig wildlife, and I vote." She leaned over the deck railing, her eyes bugged out like a grasshopper's behind those thick glasses. We could've touched noses, she was that close.

"Whatcha think? Sure is a beauty, eh?"

"Think of wha-what?"

"The snapper, honey. I call him Hogjaw. Had him for a year. Bad-tempered, but he hasn't managed to take my finger off yet." She motioned me up the stairs. "Come on in. The boy—what's his name?"

"You mean G-Gus?" I said through chattering teeth.

"That's it—Gus. He tells me you kids like sardines."

"He said what?"

"Said you all liked sardines. Kind of surprised me; I never cared a hoot for them as a kid. Anyway, I'm going to scoot back in here and rip into a can." She held the door open while I trudged up the steps, my heart still pounding. One thing for certain, if we made it out of this house without dying of food poisoning, the first thing I'd do was wring Gus Kinnard's neck.

I was making my way through the cluttered utility room, thinking how I could get Gus and Margaret outside when Margaret yelled at me from the kitchen. I poked my head through the doorway. Gus was fiddling with something on the counter and had his back to me. Margaret was sitting on the floor. When she saw me, she held a speckled brown *diapered* duck over her head. "Look. Isn't this the most adorable thing you've ever seen? A duck wearing a *diaper*. Mrs. Unger showed me how to put it on her. And she says if Doris ever has ducklings, we can each have one. Wouldn't you just love that?"

"Uh, yeah, that'd be great." I waved frantically at her behind Granny Goose's back, pointing to the door and mouthing, "Outside. I've . . . got . . . something . . . to . . . show . . . you."

Margaret cracked up laughing. She must've thought I was pointing at Pickles, who'd just popped her head through a hinged flap on the door. "Oh, look. Pickles got in the house all by herself. Isn't that cute? Did you put that little door in for her, Mrs. Unger?"

"Yep," Granny Goose said, her head buried in

the refrigerator. "It works like a doggie door. She's in and out of here all the time. Gotta watch her, though. The little bugger's not house-trained. If she runs loose without a diaper, I'll likely have a mess on my hands."

"I'll put one on her." Margaret jumped up from the floor and practically skipped to the pantry. "I'll get the halter." She was back in a flash, sitting on the kitchen floor again, before I had a chance to get her alone.

Gus set his cheese cutter down, popped a chunk of something in his mouth, then wiped his hands on his shirt. He wriggled his eyebrows at Margaret and me before turning to Granny Goose. "Mrs. Unger," he said, "so what about this Leonard guy, anyway? When he was here this morning, did he get belligerent? I mean, did he actually follow you inside? Stomp around your, uh, *kitchen*, yelling about Pickles?"

"He was in here, all right, honey. But he didn't

get too mouthy with me. He knows I'll give it right back."

"Golly. You must've been really busy this morning, Mrs. Unger," Margaret said, taking the lead from Gus. "Did you have lots of company, or was it just Leonard and François?"

Granny Goose rustled around her silverware drawer, answering Margaret as if nothing were unusual about all the questions. "Nope. They were the only two here, thank the stars. I was swamped."

Gus grinned at Margaret, giving her the thumbs-up.

Since they were having such good luck getting information, I tried my hand. "Were Leonard or François out on your deck this morning?" I asked casually.

That got raised eyebrows and a "Why, yes, they were. Why do you ask, honey?" from Granny Goose, followed by a rapid head shake and a finger to the mouth from Gus.

Ignoring him, I said, "Oh, no reason, really. I just

wondered if either of them wanted to look at your animals, maybe help you feed Hogjaw."

"Nope. No one gets in those pens but me, period. For safety reasons." She jiggled the keys hanging from her belt loop. "I keep them all locked up."

I didn't get a chance to go into more details with Granny Goose about who could've done what around Hogjaw, because my question had set her off. She started talking about her animals, and nothing short of a hurricane could've stopped her. We learned that Olive the owl had an injured wing; Charlie the gator had been run over by a car ("He's being transferred to a better-equipped reptile rescue in a couple of days," she said); Hogjaw had been found on the road with a cracked shell; and Pelly's feet had been injured when he'd landed on a piling with nails sticking out of it. "Poor little guy," Granny Goose said. "The webbing on both feet had been torn to pieces."

The more she talked about rescuing gators and owls and pelicans, the more I knew we were doing the right thing by helping her. But unless we could somehow get the egg out of the pen before Mrs. Grimstone sent the cops over, none of what we were doing would make one bit of difference.

I was mulling over the best way to accomplish that, when Granny Goose stuck four fingers between her teeth and let out an earsplitting whistle. "Didn't mean to startle you, kids. That's how I let Pickles know the chow's on. She'll pitch a fit if I don't include her."

Sure enough, it wasn't but a couple of seconds before Pickles came bopping toward the table. Her diaper had already worked itself loose, and she had a silver spoon clamped between her bill.

"Hey, kids," Granny Goose said. "My hands are full. Can somebody nab Pickles, please? She's got my serving spoon."

Gus darted across the room. "I'll get her." Pickles dodged him, heading for the hallway. Gus lunged. He grabbed the spoon and gave it to Granny Goose.

She snorted. "Honestly, what that goose won't go after. Caught her with my watch yesterday. Now sit down, kids. It's snack time."

By now my anxiety over the egg was rumbling around my stomach like a giant burp. I tapped my foot a million miles an hour as Gus poured us each a tall glass of Papaya Surprise. I motioned to Margaret to sit next to me. I had to tell her, even if it meant whispering in front of—

"Here ya go, kid." Granny Goose handed me a baking dish filled with something so heavy and green and mossy-looking I thought for sure it was Astro-turf. "It's a caramelized broccoli bake," she said. "My second choice for the cook-off contest. I'd like you to rate it against the cucumbers."

Chapter 14
Not So Clueless Anymore

I stared in horror at Granny Goose's newest green concoction.

Why me? How come she kept picking me to be her taste tester? Did I look like some kind of vegetable guru or something?

"Smells good, huh? Here. I'll cut you a nibble." She leaned over my shoulder with a bread-and-butter knife, chewing her lip and grunting as she struggled to slice the broccoli bake. She sawed away, and when she finally managed to cut a piece, she dropped it on my plate. It landed with a thud.

"It might've settled a little in the fridge, but that shouldn't affect the flavor."

I stabbed it with my fork, pretending to look interested, but wishing with all my might Gus would take it off my hands. He'd already popped a couple of sardines in his mouth like they were M&M's, and he'd been raving about the goat cheese, so why not the broccoli bake?

Gus gaped from across the table, but it wasn't the food on my plate that seemed to interest him. He was watching Pickles. She'd just climbed a miniature footstool Granny Goose had pushed up to the table. She settled herself between Margaret and me and pecked at a spoon.

"Hold your horses," Granny Goose said to Pickles. "I'll get to your plate in a second."

"Uh, Mrs. Unger, does Pickles always eat with you?" Gus said.

"You betcha. Never misses a meal. She's a vegetable lover."

My ears perked up. Pickles a vegetable lover? Hmm. Very interesting.

I casually placed my elbows on the table and asked Granny Goose if she had any salt. As soon as she turned her back to look for it, I nudged my plate to the left, close enough for Pickles to get a whiff.

Oh, happiness.

In ten seconds flat my broccoli bake was pecked into dust.

Margaret, Gus, and I doubled over laughing. Granny Goose yelled, "Bad goose!" but Pickles didn't ruffle a feather. She just sat there looking totally pleased with herself, like she was waiting on round two.

Granny Goose was all set to cut me another piece when I pushed my chair from the table and hopped up. "Uh-oh. It's after three. Golly, Mrs. Unger, I'm really sorry, but we don't have time to finish the snacks. I have to be home by three-thirty to help my mom."

Gus's fork stopped halfway to his mouth. He looked at the kitchen clock, and his eyes lit up with alarm. It was like he'd finally remembered our time crunch and that we were on an information quest, not a picnic. "Three-ten? Already? Yeah, we'd better get going. We've got lots to do."

Granny Goose wouldn't hear of our helping clean her messy kitchen. "I've enjoyed every minute of this visit," she said. "I hope you'll come back real soon."

So after Margaret paid her smoochy good-byes to Doris the duck and Pickles, we headed out the front door. We were standing on the sidewalk, waving our final farewell to Granny Goose, when Gus muttered out the side of his mouth, "Only two visitors this morning, so that concludes our suspect list."

"I can't believe it," Margaret said after the front door closed. "We've actually got this narrowed—"

"There's an egg in the turtle pen," I blurted out.

"Oh . . . my . . . gosh," Margaret said. "You mean Hogjaw laid an egg? I thought he was a boy."

"Not that kind of egg. I mean, one of the jeweled eggs."

"What?" Gus's eyes popped way open, and he stumbled backward, like he'd just seen Granny Goose's alligator slide over the fence. "Are you serious? You actually found a Pitaya in Hogjaw's pen? How come you left it there?"

"I didn't exactly *leave* it. It's wedged under a log. I couldn't reach it."

"We can't let the cops find it," Margaret said. "They'll arrest her for sure."

"That must've been the thief's plan all along," Gus said. "He was hoping someone would turn the locket in, and then, when the cops came here to search Granny Goose's, they'd find the egg."

"We have to go back for it," Margaret said.

Gus spun around. "Come on. You two keep Granny Goose busy inside, and I'll get the Pitaya."

"Wait a minute," I said. "Why would François or Leonard—whichever one did it—dump that egg? Didn't you say it was way more valuable than the locket? Why wouldn't he want to sell it?"

"That one little egg doesn't matter to the perp. He's got five more, plus all the other loot. The important thing to him is to make Granny Goose the patsy," Gus said.

We were still hashing things out when Granny Goose came back outside. She locked her front door before hurrying to the truck in her driveway. "See ya later, kids," she said, waving to us. "I'm off to the festival again. Just got an emergency call from one of the Tarts. Seems they're light on help."

She backed into the street, then stuck her head out the window. "If you need to be home by three-thirty, you'd better get a move on it, honey," she said to me. "My dashboard clock says three-seventeen."

She took off, and once her truck disappeared around the corner, Gus said, "Perfect. Let's go for it."

We raced to the backyard fence. Margaret pulled the gate handle, but it wouldn't open. Gus and I each yanked on it, too. "Darn," I said. "She must've locked it from the inside before she left."

We messed around for a couple more minutes, trying to hoist Gus, then me, then Margaret over the privacy fence, but it was way too high. And since there didn't happen to be a ten-foot extension ladder lying around anywhere, there wasn't much left to do but give up.

"We'll have to come back later," Gus said, "when she's home."

Margaret shook her head with disappointment as we crossed the lawn. "I hate to leave; it feels like we're letting Granny Goose down. What if Mrs. Grimstone sends the police over here before we get to the egg?"

"The cops can't go tromping around her backyard on a hunch. They still need probable cause. Right?" I asked Gus.

"Right, but it would've been better to take care of the egg now, to be on the safe side. Besides, there might be even more evidence in the pen."

"Wait," I said, remembering the Ford medallion. I pulled it from my pocket. "This could be evidence.

I found it under the aloe plant, right next to the turtle's log."

Gus blinked at least five times. "Holy tamale! Let me see that a minute." He took the medallion, examining it from every angle, and a grin slid across his face. "This," he said, waving it under Margaret's and my noses, "is going to be the downfall of our perp."

Chapter 15
Partner Problems

We all agreed on one thing: The medallion belonged to the thief.

Gus said the odds were high. "At least eighty-five percent. Because Granny Goose drives a Honda, and she doesn't let anyone else in the animal pens."

"Leonard and François were both on her deck this morning," I said. "All we have to do is find out who owns a Ford."

"I know François drives a red convertible," Margaret said. "I've seen him in it. But I don't know the make."

"What about Leonard? We saw him in that truck earlier. Was it a Ford?" I said.

Gus shrugged. "I didn't notice. We'll have to track both of them down."

"Hey, I know what. Let's go by François' café. Maybe his car is parked there," Margaret said.

Gus and her got all excited over that idea, and I would've gotten excited, too, if I hadn't lived in the opposite direction from Simply Paris. And according to Margaret's watch, it was three-twenty. When my mom says to be home at three-thirty, she doesn't mean three thirty-two. Plus she'd been planning this festival schedule for months, down to the minute. If I messed her up now, I wouldn't get out of the house for the rest of the week.

"I can't. I've got to dice cucumbers. I've only got ten minutes to get home."

I was waiting for Margaret to say, "I'll help you; then we'll meet back up with Gus when we're done."

But she didn't. Instead, she started planning things out with him, about where they would go and when. No mention of Lindy. I swallowed hard, disappointment stuck in my throat like catfish bones. A wave of jealousy flooded my chest, because what if they figured things out without me?

We started down the sidewalk, and as Gus mapped out their plans, I ground my teeth in frustration. It'd been me, not him, who'd found the locket and the Pitaya egg and the key ring. But the way he was acting, you would've thought he was the one who'd discovered everything.

And another thing. Margaret was supposed to be my best friend. At least that's the way it'd been for the last six years. So why was she acting like Gus's best friend? Why hadn't she offered to help me with my festival chores, like I always helped her with stuff?

I was stewing over this when a car turned into the driveway we were approaching, just two houses down from Granny Goose's. Cricket from Shear Magic jumped out. She looked at us curiously, then gave a quick hello flick with her finger.

"Listen," Margaret whispered to me, because we

were within earshot of Cricket. "Gus and I'll check Simply Paris for François' car, then come back here and see if Granny Goose is home. I'll call you later and tell you everything. And hurry! I know how your mom is. I don't want you to get in trouble for being late."

I made it home with one minute to spare, still steaming at Margaret and Gus. I knew it wasn't fair for me to be mad. After all, we'd made a pact to help Granny Goose and earn that reward, so they were doing the right thing by working without me. And I really, really wanted the money. Why then, I wondered, did I keep feeling like I'd lost my best friend?

Things weren't any better at the Phillips residence. Besides having to peel and chop two hundred cucumbers, good old Lindy got stuck with Henry for the whole night. That's because Dad got called into the fire station, and Mom had scheduled herself to work the senior square dance at the festival.

"I won't be home until nine," she told me. "I'd

take Henry with me, but he's been complaining of a tummy ache."

"It's because of those stupid stewed cucumbers," he grumbled from under the kitchen table. "They made me get diarrhea so bad I almost died."

I leaned over and looked at him. His cheeks were pudgy and pink as ever, his brown eyes twinkled, and he was surrounded by Matchbox cars and Spider-Man action figures. He sure didn't look sick to me.

But none of that mattered, because Mom was in too big of a hurry to listen to any arguments. "You can take Henry to the Quick Mart for a SevenUP later," she said. "That always helps his tummy. Otherwise, I want him to stay in. Make sure he gets to bed by eight."

So there you go. One whole evening of peeling and chopping and playing board games with Henry. After the third round of Boggle Junior, I called Margaret.

No answer, just like the last ten times I called. I tried Gus's house. He wasn't home either.

It was six o'clock, and I still hadn't heard a thing.

After the fifth round of old maid with Henry, I was so antsy I wanted to chew the cards up and spit them out the window. I paced the living room, and then a plan came to me. An excellent plan.

Ha! I didn't need Margaret or Gus. I'd do some investigative work on my own. Since they had supposedly checked François' make of car, I'd take care of Leonard. I grabbed the phone book. "Snout, Leonard: 1212 South Rural Route 3."

I couldn't use our phone, because Leonard might have caller ID. My mom claimed everyone had caller ID. "It's the best thing the phone company's ever come out with," she'd told my dad.

"Hey," I said to Henry, "you want to go to Quick Mart for a SevenUP now?"

That was like asking Bugs Bunny if he wanted a carrot. While Henry dashed upstairs for his shoes, I memorized Leonard's phone number.

Chapter 16
Getting Nowhere Fast

Five minutes later I was at the pay phone outside Quick Mart, watching Henry through the window. "You can get a SevenUP and some gum and one more treat," I'd said, hoping to keep him in there for a while, "but do . . . *not* . . . disappear from my sight."

I dropped my coins into the slot. This isn't a prank call, I told myself. It's more like a business call. But my hands shook so hard I could hardly punch the numbers.

Leonard picked up on the third ring. "Hello?"

"Yes. Uh, hello, sir." I held a sock I'd brought with me over the mouthpiece, so he wouldn't recognize my voice. "This is Monica Wilson. Our company is conducting a survey about vehicular models, and I'd like to know—"

"You're doing a what?"

"A *survey*, sir. About vehicular models that people drive."

"What the heck you trying to sell me?" Leonard grumbled.

"Actually, sir, I'm not selling anything." I chuckled, trying to act all buddy, buddy with him. "Everyone thinks that. What we're doing is conducting a national survey. We'd like to know what kind of vehicle you drive."

"Tell me again what you're after," Leonard said. "You're sounding fuzzy on my end."

"Certainly. Our—"

A car honked, practically blasting my ear off.

"What?" Leonard said.

Uh-oh. Henry was headed my way, his arms full. I had to get off this phone. What if he saw me, and, like he always did, shouted, "Who are you talking to, Lindy?" Leonard might hear him.

"What . . . kind . . . of . . . ve-hic-le . . . do . . . you . . . drive?" I yelled into the receiver. Just hurry up and answer me already, I wanted to say.

"Ford," Leonard said. "I've had it ten years. Wouldn't buy anything else."

"Thank you." I hung up the phone in time to see Henry spill his fountain drink all over the floor.

The telephone message light was blinking when Henry and I finally made it home.

"Where *are* you, Lindy?" Margaret's voice said. "Call me right away! I've got N-E-W-S."

"News about what?" Henry said. He stuffed another Gummi Bear in his mouth. This from the boy with the killer stomachache.

I shooed him upstairs. "Get the Monopoly game out," I said, "and we'll play before bedtime."

When I called Margaret back, she was talking so fast and loud I had to hold the phone away from my ear. "Guess! What? Ohmigosh, you'll never guess what, Lindy! François drives a Mustang. A *Ford* Mustang. And Gus says the more he thought about it, the more he thought Leonard drives a Chevy, so now we almost know for sure who the thief is."

"No, you don't," I said, "because Gus is wrong. Leonard does drive a Ford." I went on to tell her about *my* discovery, and I was feeling all proud and pleased with myself until I realized that since they both drove Fords, we weren't any closer to guessing the thief than we'd been six hours ago.

Another bad thing was that Margaret and Gus hadn't been able to get the egg. "My parents saw us and made me take Sarah and Carrie"—that's Margaret's little twin sisters—"on the midway rides, so Gus went to Granny Goose's by himself. But she still wasn't home. She was playing fiddle for the senior square dance on the courthouse lawn. I saw her."

This meant we hadn't accomplished anything the whole day, unless you want to count learning how to put a diaper on a goose as progress. I hadn't felt this blue in a long time. Not only was Granny Goose in danger of being caught with the egg, but we were no closer to winning that reward.

And then, with one final tidbit of information, Margaret turned my blue mood into a deep gray funk. "Mr. Austin called my mom. He wants Gus and me to play a trio with Angel in the festival finale Saturday afternoon. It's the same song that you, me, and Gus played at the spring concert."

"But what about me?" I said. My voice sounded small and whiny, just like Henry's after he'd spilled his 7UP. "Does Mr. Austin want me to play, too?"

"Well, this is what really makes me mad. He said it's supposed to be just Gus, me, and Angel, all because she wants to play that same solo part you had. Since she's the Festival Princess, he wants to highlight her on the flute. I didn't want to do it, but my mom told him yes. And we have to rehearse at ten in the morning, too. So we won't be free until eleven."

I could barely force the words "Okay, yeah, well, see you tomorrow" out of my mouth before hanging up. I sat there for a full minute, staring at the wall, not wanting to believe what I'd just heard: Margaret and Gus were going to play "Melody from the South Seas," my favorite song in the world, with Angel Grimstone. Without me. And the Princess would be playing *my* solo part, the very same solo I could play with my eyes closed.

"Hurry up, Lindy," Henry yelled from upstairs. "We've only got an hour to play Monopoly before bedtime."

I trudged up the stairs to join him, feeling numb. For the first time ever, I didn't even yell, "Dibs on being the banker."

Chapter 17
Conspiracy Theory

The next morning I got up early, before Henry. I decided to make a list of what we needed to do to get Granny Goose off the hook and find the thief. I'd been at it for a half hour, but so far the only thing I'd come up with was: "Get jeweled egg out of Hogjaw's pen." I still didn't know how to accomplish this. Granny Goose would probably be at the festival most of the day, and even if I stopped by for a "casual" visit at seven o'clock in the morning, it's not like I could poke around Hogjaw's pen right in front of her.

As much as I hated to think it, I needed Gus's help. He had a knack for drawing up plans; I was better at uncovering evidence. I was supposed to meet him and Margaret after their rehearsal and get started from there, but Mom nixed that plan. "I need your help in the cucumber smoothie booth from ten until noon," she said, "and then again from three until five."

"What?" I stared at her with my mouth hanging open. Hadn't I done enough already? I was probably the only kid in town who'd ever peeled and chopped two hundred cucumbers.

"You'll have plenty of free time in between," she said.

I got to the square a few minutes early, hoping to find Margaret or Gus and tell them I'd be working for Mom, and that's when I saw Leonard.

And François.

They were standing together next to the elephant ear stand. Leonard had on those same farmer overalls and straw hat. François was wearing a spotless white apron; his mustache looked sleek and perfectly curled. He pointed to a cluster of flowers in front of the courthouse and started jabbering away to Leonard. Then his hands flew all over the place, like he was excited about something.

Holy cow! Did these two know each other? Were they actually friends? No, I thought as I watched them. Somehow, I couldn't picture them as buddies. It would be like mixing powdered sugar with sour milk.

I edged closer to the stand. Maybe I could hear what they were talking about. Trying to act casual, I bought a cinnamon elephant ear. I munched on it as I leaned against the side of the food trailer.

But I couldn't make out what they were saying. I'd have to get closer. Not too close, otherwise Leonard might recognize me. He might connect me with last night's phone call. I sidled toward them, holding the elephant ear in front of my face. I licked the cinnamon topping, tilted my head in their direction. My heart raced.

"*Non, non.* That is not the prime location to place it, my friend. *Certainement—oui,* certainly, the Pitaya requires direct sunlight, for the maximum—"

I gagged . . . coughed . . . sputtered . . . nearly choked to death on a chunk of elephant ear. Leonard looked over at me, and our eyes played tag for one short second. I ducked around the other side of the food booth. Now my heart was pounding.

"Hey, Lindy!" Henry waved at me from down the street. "Come on. Mom says I get to help you make the smoothies. She's going to show us how."

By ten forty-five, Henry and I had a line. A constant *whirr, whirr, whirr* of cucumbers, lime juice, sugar, and ice spun around my blender like a funnel cloud. For the life of me, I couldn't figure why anyone in his right mind would line up for one of these drinks, especially when he could've had a lemon shake-up or a strawberry milk shake.

At least we were busy, which made the time go fast. But nothing—not even the long line or making change or Henry's constant jabber—could take my mind off that one word François had said: *Pitaya*. I couldn't wait to tell Margaret and Gus what I'd overheard.

They showed up at around eleven. "We've been looking all over for you," Margaret said, practically breathless with excitement. "Guess what Gus found out."

I checked my line: seven people waiting, and Henry was the only helper. "You go ahead and pour this man's drink," I told him. "I'll just be a second."

I grabbed Margaret's arm. "You're not going to believe what I—"

"Tell her, Gus!" she squealed. "Tell her what you figured out."

"Lindeeee, I need help," Henry whined.

"Shh!" I hissed over my shoulder. "You can pour it yourself. There's enough in the pitcher for three more servings. Just take two dollars or two tickets from each customer; that's all you have to do. If you need to make change, I'll be right here."

"I've got big news," Gus said, wriggling his

eyebrows. "Really, really big." Margaret cracked up laughing.

"So do I," I said, but Gus just blasted right ahead, like what I had to say didn't matter.

"It's a conspiracy," he announced. "Leonard and François. François and Leonard. I saw them together this morning, and I'm ninety percent sure they're working as a team."

What the heck? That was supposed to be my news.

"Get . . . out!" Margaret said after I'd told them my story. "They were actually talking about the Pitaya?" She looked at Gus, wide-eyed, like she'd never been so amazed about anything in her life. "It's exactly what you thought," she whispered. "Exactly. You do have ESP."

"Yep. It's like I told you, I could tell by their body language." And then he started up with the NSCCB stuff again . . . on and on about how he'd "deciphered subtle innuendos" to win crime buster of the month, and brag, brag, brag about he'd interpreted the clues, until I had to clamp down on my tongue to keep from saying anything.

"What time will you be done here?" Margaret said. "Gus and I have to rehearse again at eleven thirty."

"I thought you just got done rehearsing."

"We did. But Mr. Austin feels it needs some more work." She didn't say it, but I knew without asking that Gus was the problem.

"We'll be done at noon," Gus said. "Wanna meet up back here? I went over my NSCCB notes last night. I've got a couple of ideas."

"Okay." And they'd better be darn good ones, I thought, because we were running out of time.

"LinDEEE!" Henry cried from behind me. "It's not my fault. It was an accident."

Chapter 128
The Tattletale Threat

A gooey lake of spilled smoothie covered our booth counter. It dribbled into the money box—*drip, drip, drip*—and coated my mom's master festival schedule.

Henry's T-shirt and shorts were soaked, and our line had grown to at least ten grim-faced, restless customers.

I'd barely managed to get things under control and whip up another blender of drinks before my mom showed back up. "I need you to run an errand, Lindy," she said, and for once I didn't care what it involved. By then I was so sticky and hot and tired of looking at cucumbers, I would've gladly cleaned a whole row of Porta Potties.

"Evelyn left something on her front porch," Mom said. "She'll be working the Tarts' tent until tonight and won't have time to run back for it, so I offered your services."

Go to Granny Goose's? My heart fluttered. Maybe, just maybe, her back gate would be unlocked and I could take care of that egg. "Uh, sure. What does she want?"

"She needs you to grab the gym bag on her porch. Evidently, François left it at her house yesterday."

François' gym bag? Wow. This was getting even better. Suppose I found another heirloom inside it, or some secret correspondence between him and Leonard. I took off in an excited rush, but I wasn't a block away before my adrenaline fizzled out. I couldn't quit thinking that once again Margaret and Gus—my supposed partners—weren't with me, and once again I was operating by myself.

When I got to Granny Goose's, I hurried to her

back gate. Still locked. It didn't look like we'd ever get in there, at least until the Festival was over. But that might be way too late, especially after what Mrs. Grimstone had said about calling the police.

I swallowed my disappointment and headed up the porch steps. François' bag was sitting next to the front door. With trembling hands, I unzipped and emptied it onto the porch floor. Here's what I found:

- Merlin's Moustache Wax: "Works like Magic for that Sleek, Sexy Look."
- A tube of BriteSmile toothpaste and a toothbrush.
- About twenty-five of the fliers advertising his vegetable carving show.
- About one hundred fliers advertising a special breakfast on Saturday.
- A plain white T-shirt.
- A pair of slinky gold boxer shorts with a swirly F stitched on them.

Drat. Not one tiny piece of evidence. Feeling even more discouraged, I stuffed everything back in the bag and took off down Citrus Grove. Cricket was outside the same house we'd seen her at yesterday, pulling some bags out of her car trunk. "Hey," she said. "Back again, eh? You're sure spending a lot of time in the neighborhood these days."

She pulled off her sunglasses and stared at me.

"Oh," I answered with a nervous giggle, "I'm just running an errand for Granny Goo—I mean Mrs. Unger. Um . . . do you live here?"

"Last time I checked. Hey, are you okay, kid? You look a little freaked out."

"I'm fine. Really. Just in kind of a hurry."

"Wait a minute. You aren't after that goose of hers, are you?" Cricket looked up and down the sidewalk before backing against her car. "I can't stand that thing. It tried to bite me yesterday."

"I'm not looking for Pickles. It's . . . well, I'm . . ."

I'm not sure what made me keep talking. Maybe it was the way Cricket seemed so hip and cool and unadultish, or maybe the thought that she had inside information about the heirloom theft. After all, she knew Mrs. Grimstone; she'd even been at her house yesterday, talking about the crime.

Cricket tilted her head and looked at me expectantly, so I went on. "Do you know anything about the heirloom robbery?"

Her eyebrows shot up. "Like what?"

"Well, uh . . . . do you know if . . . uh . . ." Just say it, Lindy. I took a deep breath. "Does Mrs. Grimstone really think Mrs. Unger stole those heirlooms? Has she called the cops?"

"Oh, now I get it. You kids are playing detective."

I fidgeted with François' bag, feeling a hot blush creep up my cheeks.

"We kind of accidentally overheard something."

"Okay, what gives here, Libby?"

"Lindy. My name's Lindy. And nothing gives. I'm just worried about Mrs. Unger. My friends and I know she can't be the thief. From what we've found—

I mean, from what we, uh, *think*, someone else must've done it."

Cricket's dark red lips parted into a curious smile. She opened a SureFresh wintergreen mint container and popped one in her mouth, watching me the whole time. "You got any other suspects?"

"Well," I said, lowering my voice, "the Grimstones' gardener is a little mysterious, don't you think?" I was hoping my confidential attitude would get her to talk. Maybe she'd seen Leonard snooping around the Grimstones' and suspected he was up to something.

"You got that right," Cricket said. "It wouldn't shock me one bit if that creep and the goose lady are in on it to—never mind. Forget I said that. Just stay out of it, okay? I don't want to see you kids get hurt."

"What about Mrs. Grimstone? What does she think?"

"Look, I'm not at liberty to discuss anything Mrs. Grimstone confides in me, seeing as how I'm her personal hairstylist and all. That would be a breach of confidence."

I nodded, trying for an "oh-yes-I-totally-comprehend-what-you're-saying" look, even though I wasn't real clear on her point. It's not like I was asking if Mrs. Grimstone dyed her hair or wore false eyelashes.

Cricket put her hands on her hips. She studied me for several seconds, making me squirm in my flip-flops. So much for my thinking she was unadultish. I could already hear the lecture working its way up her voice box.

"Listen," she said, "I'm not trying to be the bad guy here. But I'm warning you, if I see you kids snooping around where you could get hurt, I'll have a little discussion with your mother at her hair appointment this coming Monday. Got it?"

Oh, yeah. I got it all right. Cricket was going to rat on me. I backed away from her, muttering, "We'll stay out of trouble. I promise." I hurried back down Citrus Grove, hoping that by Monday she'd have forgotten our encounter.

Margaret and Gus were waiting behind the smoothie stand when I got back.

Mom took François' bag from me. "Thanks for going after this, sweetie. You can deliver it to Simply Paris in a minute, but first, I have another favor to ask." She handed me some festival tickets. "I'm parched, and these smoothies don't begin to quench my thirst. Can you get me a lemon shake-up? And then you'll be free until three o'clock, I promise."

As soon as we took off, I told Margaret and Gus how I'd checked inside François' gym bag, and about my conversation with Cricket.

Did they praise me? Did either of them say, "Wow! Great investigating, Lindy"? Nope. Just a couple of surprised looks and maybe an "ooh" or two from Margaret. And then Gus barked out a bunch of statistics and crime lingo about perps and patsies and buncos. He went on and on about what we should do next, not even asking my opinion, even though I'm the one who'd found every single piece of evidence so far. But what really bugged me was the way Margaret agreed with everything he said, as if he were one of the Hardy Boys or something. It went like this:

Gus: "Here's the thing"—blah, blah, blah . . .

Margaret: "Great idea"—yada, yada, yada . . .

Gus: "And another thing"—blah, blah, blah . . .

Margaret: "Great idea"—yada, yada, yada . . .

Me: Nothing. Because I couldn't get a word in edgewise.

I was ready to yell, "Let me say something here, please," when a noise crackled from the loudspeakers, like teeth scraping over metal. It was the Cucumber Princess, onstage with a swarm of kids from school. She had the microphone up to her mouth, and she must've had the volume set on full blast, because when she screeched, "Oh, lookie, lookie. Here comes Lindy Loopy with her true love, Snoopy," you could've heard her all the way in North Dakota.

Chapter 19
Friendship Fiasco

Angel's voice blared from the loudspeakers again, even louder this time. "Oh, puh-leeeze, Lindy Loopy. Give your sexy-phone player a great big kiss for us." She doubled up over the mike, cackling.

You could've roasted a marshmallow over my cheeks. Gus stood between Margaret and me, stiff and silent. I was pretty sure that like me, he'd stopped breathing.

"Ignore her," Margaret whispered.

I yanked my shoulders back and took a step toward the stage.

"Come on, Lindy," Margaret said under her breath.

She tugged my arm. "Let's go. Don't get in a fight with her. Remember the trouble you got in last time?"

I did remember—a trip to the principal's office, to be exact—and I should've taken Margaret's advice. But she wasn't the one who'd just been totally mortified by Angel Grimstone.

The words flew out of my mouth before I could stop them.

"Ha-ha! That's pretty funny, especially since *you're* the one who wanted him to squeak along in your stupid trio. That must mean it's *you*, not me, who's got the crush on him!"

Oh, no. Had I just shouted that? In front of all those people? The blood drained from my face. I felt dizzy, sick to my stomach. I stole a peek at Gus from the corner of my eye. His face looked white and sad and twitchy, like he'd just lost his best friend.

He backed away from us.

"Don't go," Margaret said. "Lindy didn't mean it."

Her eyes flashed with anger when she said, "Did you?"

I shook my head and sputtered a few no's and sorry's, but I couldn't bring myself to look at him again. I felt too bad.

"You can't leave," Margaret said as Gus took another backward step. "We haven't figured out who"—she checked over her shoulder before dropping her voice—"you-know-what."

"Never mind," Gus said. "Forget it. You guys can solve it without me."

"But what about the show tomorrow?" Margaret said. "I don't want to play a duet with Angel."

"I told Mr. Austin I'd do it, so I'll be there," Gus said, and then he was gone.

"Where's Gussy going, Lindy?" Angel yelled from the stage. "Did you have a fight?"

On a normal day, I would've snatched her tiara and stomped it into tinfoil. But this wasn't a normal day, and there were way too many people around. So I said something lame like "Ho-ho-ho. You're a regular comedian," and Margaret said, "Shut up, Angel," and then the two of us wove our way through the crowd, away from the stage.

Margaret kept scanning the lawn, looking for Gus. "I don't see him anywhere."

I shrugged, trying to act like it wasn't a big deal. "Maybe he went after a balloon hat or something."

"No, he's gone, and I don't blame him. How come you treated him like that, anyway?"

"Me? It's not my fault. Angel's the one who started it. I just didn't want everyone to think he's my boyfriend."

Little splotches of red dotted Margaret's cheeks. "Gosh, Lindy. Just because you don't want him for a boyfriend doesn't mean you can't be nice to him. He's lots of fun. And he's really smart, too."

"At least he *thinks* he's smart."

"He *is* smart." Margaret plunked her hands on her hips. "You know what? I think you're jealous because Gus is figuring out everything about the heirlooms before you do."

"Are you kidding? I'm the one who found all the evidence, not Gus."

"But he's the only one who knows what to do with it. I wish he was still here. We'll never solve this without him." She kicked at a cluster of pebbles, then plopped down on the street curb.

I didn't say it, but I was starting to think the same thing. And in a weird kind of way, I already missed Gus. Maybe I'd grown attached to his corny sense of humor, or that funny-looking cowlick, or the way he was always quoting NSCCB facts. But now I'd gone and totally screwed things up, and he'd probably never speak to me again.

Chapter 20
François Flips Out

After delivering Mom's drink and picking up the gym bag, Margaret and I headed for Simply Paris. We'd walked only a half block or so before she said, "You've got to call him, you know. You've got to apologize."

I nodded, but I had a sinking feeling in my gut, the kind you get after realizing you've messed up every single percentage problem on the big math test, and you've already turned it in. Because some things you just can't go back and fix.

And how, exactly, would I phrase an apology to Gus?

"Please forgive me. I'm really truly sorry I said that . . ."

Or . . . "It's all Angel's fault, you know . . ."

Or maybe something kind of casual, like . . . "Yo. Chill, dude. It's really no big—"

"Watch out, Lindy!" Margaret yanked my arm, saving me from a face-to-face crash with François Pouppière. Actually, it wasn't the real François; it was a life-size wooden cutout of him, standing in the middle of the sidewalk. He was holding a sign that said:

BLOOMSBERRIANS . . . HURRAY! IT'S YOUR LUCKY DAY!

MEET FRANÇOIS, THE CHEF BEHIND THE SMILE

AND VEGETABLE SCULPTOR EXTRAORDINAIRE!

ENJOY A COOL DRINK AT SIMPLY PARIS,

WHILE THE AMAZING FRANÇOIS DEMONSTRATES HOW TO:

DICE, SLICE, AND FLEURETTE!!

TODAY AT 1:00 P.M.

SPECIAL FESTIVAL PRICE: ONLY $35 PER GUEST

At least twenty old ladies were gathered outside the restaurant, yakking away as they waited for the doors to open.

Margaret and I made our way through them and turned down the alley, following a strong scent of garlic and onion toward the Simply Paris kitchen. Accordion music blared from an open window, along with clattering pots and pans and people talking. I was all set to knock on the kitchen door, yet feeling nervous about facing François, when a voice blasted through the window. "ARRETEZ-VOUS! HALT! CEASE EVERYTHING—*IMMEDIATEMENT!*"

All the noise, even the accordion music, stopped. Margaret clutched my wrist. We flattened ourselves against the outside of the building, right under the window.

"*Intrus!*" François said. "Yes, an intrusion . . . into my private office . . . *Mon Dieu*, it's an outrage! *Jamais*—never, I announce—will I tolerate such insubordination. Whosoever is the culprit, *montrez-vous!* Speak up, I say."

Dead silence inside. All I heard was Margaret's and my heavy breathing.

"Very well"—François went on—"if no one is to admit the guilt, I shall establish a dire warning. From this very moment and hereafter, the first employee who dares enter my office without permission is terminated from Simply Paris employment." It sounded like he slammed something onto a counter, and then the music came back on.

"Now back to work, back to work," François sang out. "*Immédiatement*, if you please. I have cucumbers to carve."

I wiped my brow, still dazed by his outburst. "Jeez," I whispered, "I sure wouldn't want to be the person who ever got caught in his office."

"Me either." Margaret's eyes were wide with alarm. She nodded at the gym bag. "Let's just leave that, okay?" We set it outside the screen door and hurried toward the far end of the Simply Paris patio, where our alley intersected with another, next to a small parking lot.

We were talking about how unpredictable

François seemed—mad as a hatter one minute, all kissy-kissy the next—when Margaret pointed to a shiny red convertible in the parking lot. The license tag said "#1 François." "That's his car. Gus and I saw it out here yesterday."

I ambled over to the car. The convertible top was down. Books and papers were strewn across the seats.

"What're you doing?" Margaret said as I leaned over the side and into the backseat. "Be careful. What if he comes outside?"

"He's got a bunch of stuff in here. We might find some evidence."

Margaret checked over her shoulder, then inched toward the car. "You can't go through his stuff. That's against the law."

"Well, it's way more against the law to steal heirlooms and frame an innocent person," I said. "And that's exactly what François is guilty of. I even heard him talking about the Pitaya, remember?"

I picked up a stack of papers, causing her to throw her hands over her mouth and squeak like a mouse. A small black notebook fell onto the seat. Etched in silver on the cover, it said "Daily Planner of François Pouppière."

Chapter 21
Parlez-vous français?

My hands shook as I opened the planner. I thumbed through it quickly, flipping all the way to June.

"What does it say?" Margaret scooted closer to me, peering over my shoulder.

"I don't know. It's in French."

We stood next to François' car, scouring every day of June, looking for English words. Margaret pointed to "Grimstone" and "Unger," and I thought that's all we had, until I saw "Pitayas" under Tuesday, June 14. "Look," I said, pointing it out.

"Ohmigosh. It's the eggs! He means the eggs."

"We've got to keep this." I slipped it into my pocket.

Margaret stared at me, wide-eyed. "Are you serious?"

"Of course I am. It's no worse than hiding the locket, is it? It's only a little notebook. It might lead us to the heirlooms."

"But we can't read French."

"There's a program on the Web we can use. All we have to do is type in the French words and it translates them."

"What about Gus?" Margaret said.

"What about him?" I felt my neck growing warm.

"He can translate the French a lot faster than we can. Besides, we have to tell him what happened. You can't leave him out, Lindy. That's not fair."

She was right, of course. I knew Gus was fluent in French because he'd bragged about it hundreds of times at school. Except now I had one gigantic problem. Gus wasn't speaking to me, and I doubted that he still wanted to be our partner.

Before we left the parking lot, I decided to get one last look in François' car. I leaned way over the door and was shuffling through more papers on the floor when Margaret whispered, "*Psst!* Here comes Cricket out the back of Shear Magic."

I sprang straight up, just in time to see her cross the alley.

"Oh, uh, hi," I said, brushing off my legs.

Cricket stopped. She popped a SureFresh mint in her mouth, staring at me the whole time. "Hey, what's up? You two looking for something?"

The perky smile on her face seemed more curious than anything. But the tilt of her head, the glint in her eye . . . that's what Gus would call body language, for sure. And what Cricket's body language said to me was, "Watch out, Lindy Phillips. I know you just swiped something from François' car, and you're headed for trouble, because I'm going to tell your mom what you're up to the first chance I get."

"Yes, as a matter of fact, we are looking for something," Margaret said. She picked up a handful of fliers from the convertible's backseat and flashed her most innocent smile. "These. We're helping François distribute them for his breakfast tomorrow."

Cricket's gaze flitted from me to Margaret, then back to me. Her eyes stayed squinted, doubtful, but all she said was, "Sounds like a plan." And then she headed across the parking lot toward her car.

"Come on," I said to Margaret. "Let's go translate this planner."

We made it to my house in ten minutes flat. The good news was that Henry and my parents weren't around, so no one was using the computer. The bad news was that Margaret and I wouldn't be using it either. Because it wouldn't turn on. I pressed the "on" key at least fifty times. Nothing. Then I punched every single button on the keyboard. Still nothing.

"Let's go to your house," I said.

Margaret shook her head. "Can't. My mom's got company, and they'll all be in the family room. Besides, she won't allow me on it, anyway. I'm restricted to half an hour in the evening."

We sat on the sofa, listening to the *tick, tick, tick* of Mom's grandfather clock in the hallway. Pixie purred on my lap. After silently counting along for thirty-six straight ticks, I took the phone from its cradle. I had to call Gus, no matter how awkward it felt. He'd been our partner from the very beginning, we needed him now, and it was my fault, not Margaret's, he wasn't here. I never should've said any of that to Angel. I should've stuck up for Gus. That's what a real friend would do.

I punched in the numbers, then put the phone to my ear.

Chapter 22
Translation = Suspicions Confirmed

I held tight to the receiver, my hands slick with sweat. I'd almost rather have called Leonard Snout again.

One ring: My knee bounced up and down, up and down.

Two rings: The knot in my stomach felt tight and twisty, like a ball of rubber bands.

Three rings: Come on, Gus. Where are you?

He answered on the fourth.

"Hi," I said, trying to sound as bubbly and friendly as Margaret. "Where'd you go today?"

"Nowhere."

Hmm . . . this wasn't going so well. "You want to hear what happened after you took off?"

Silence.

"Uh, well, Margaret and I found something."

I waited for him to ask what, but all I heard was a TV in the background.

"François' daily planner," I said.

"So?"

So? Jeez. Couldn't he at least give me more than a one-word answer?

"So," I said, "it might have important information."

"What do you mean 'it might'? Haven't you read it yet?"

Aha. Now he sounded interested. I smiled and nodded at Margaret. She was chewing on her thumbnail, watching me.

"We can't read it because it's in French."

No answer.

"Well?" I said.

"Well what?"

"Well, *two* things," I said, taking a deep breath. "We need you to translate the French in the planner, and . . . the only reason I said all that to Angel is I was jealous because I didn't get chosen for the trio. And I promise I didn't mean any of it, especially about the squeaking. And I'm really, really sorry."

"Oh, man," he said, and right then, right there, I could feel his NSCCB vibrations pulsing through the telephone lines. "You're brilliant! The daily planner? That's a spectacular find. One hundred percent cool. I'll meet you guys at the midway, by the bingo tent."

We sat at a picnic table under the blazing afternoon sun. Gus was squished between Margaret and me like a pig in a blanket, and all three of us were munching kettle corn, slugging lemon shake-ups, and poring over François' scribbles. Every ten seconds a man in the tent next to us would holler something like "Under the *B*, ladies and gentlemen, it's beeee . . . six," and I thought how much easier it would be to win that bingo jackpot than figure out this mess called François' planner.

Even Gus was having a hard time. "Man," he said, "his handwriting's terrible. I can hardly read this." I didn't say anything, but I was starting to wonder if he was as fluent in French as he'd claimed.

Starting at Wednesday, June 1, Gus traced his finger down the pages, muttering random words and phrases to himself: "'*couteaux d'ordre*' . . . order knives . . . '*preparez la crème de citron—tôt*' . . . prepare lemon custard—early."

"Got something," he announced, stopping on Monday, June 6. "Here, François says '*téléphoné à L Snout—jardinier des fleurs du Grimstones*.' That means 'call L Snout, the Grimstones' flower gardener.' And look here"—he showed us an arrow that led to one word in the margin—"'*disposé*?' That means 'willing,'" Gus said, "like François wonders if Leonard is willing to do something."

My heart pattered. "Keep going."

Gus fumbled over the entry for Tuesday, June 7. "It's messy, hard to read, but I think it says, 'Book airline ticket—Air France. Depart June 20.'" Then he sucked in a huge breath. "Holy tamale! Wait'll you hear what's next."

"What?" Margaret and I said together.

"On Wednesday, June 8, François says, 'Contact Rousseau. Still in Paris?' Then it says 'How . . . much . . . for G's . . . diamond?' Yep! That's it, all right. 'How much for G's diamond?' I'm ninety-eight percent sure of it."

Margaret spewed a mouthful of kettle corn into her hand. "Oh . . . my . . . gosh. G means Grimstone. He's going to sell Mrs. Grimstone's diamonds in Paris."

"Yeah, Rousseau's his Paris fence all right," Gus said.

"Fence?" I said.

"Yeah. It's the guy who buys the stolen goods; happens in about sixty percent of theft cases. So, now we know our perp's got a fence. That's good for us, though. It means he's still holding everything, so we've got time to find out where."

I reached behind Gus and gave Margaret a high five. Finally, we had some hard evidence against François and Leonard.

Gus read more random words and phrases, like 'new boxers' and 'restock pantry,' but his finger stopped, and his eyes flew open at Tuesday, June 14. "Here's something good. This says, "'1 P.M. Tarts' soufflé at G's. L to work!'"

"What's that mean?" I said.

"Simple," Gus said. "Tuesday was the soufflé demonstration, the day Mrs. Grimstone thinks she got robbed. Here's how it went down: The Grimstones' house was open; François was keeping everyone busy in the kitchen. So that's when Leonard went to work, as in *pulled off the heist*. Man, those guys are slick."

"But what about Mr. Grimstone?" Margaret said. "Wouldn't he have been home?"

"No." I shook my head, because the Grimstones' porch conversation had come back to me.
"Mr. Grimstone was away Tuesday, remember? He
didn't even know about the soufflé thing."

"François and Leonard must've known he'd be
gone," Gus said. He turned back to the planner. Two
seconds later he slammed it on the table and whistled.
"Hot dog! We got 'em! We got 'em good. Look."

To me, it looked like a bunch of random letters, like something Henry had scribbled: '*Téléphoné
au contact de Snout—Combien serrait la valeur des
pitayas?*' But Gus was bouncing and whooping like
he'd just uncovered a mummy.

"What?" I said, tugging at his sleeve. "What does
it mean?"

"It means I'm a hundred and ninety percent sure
we're right, that's what, 'cause it says, 'Call Snout's
contact—How much are the Pitayas worth?'"

Chapter 23
Plotting and Planning

"Get . . . out." Margaret stared at Gus in amazement, lemon juice dribbling down her chin.

"Here's another Wednesday, June 15 entry." Gus hunched back over the planner and squinted. " '*Appelez le serrurier.*' Hmm . . . Oh, I got it! It means 'call the' . . . um . . . I'm pretty sure it's *locksmith*. And then it says 'office and pantry.' Yep." Gus leaned back in his seat. "That's what it says. Sounds like he needs better locks, huh? Makes you wonder why, like maybe he's storing something *valuable* back there?"

Margaret and I looked at each other in shock. I told Gus about the fit François had thrown earlier.

"This is making perfect sense," Gus said. "He's paranoid, a normal reaction for a perp. Actually, paranoia strikes at least eighty percent of all criminals. And our man is definitely freaked out. No doubt about it, he's got heirlooms hidden at Simply Paris."

Excitement zipped through my body. Even my toenails tingled. It all fitted together: the airline ticket, the locksmith, the meeting with Leonard, the Paris connection, the Pitaya contact . . . on and on.

"Wait," Gus said, his finger in the air, his nose to the planner again. "One last entry. According to this, on Saturday, June 18, there's a staff meeting on the patio from eight-thirty until eight forty-five, before the breakfast." He closed the planner and grinned. "That's tomorrow morning, and guess who's gonna be there?"

Margaret hiccuped. "Us?"

"Yep. It's the perfect opportunity. We'll let ourselves in through the kitchen door, check things out while François is holding his meeting. Seventh guideline, NSCCB: Double-check what you can. Seventy-five percent of mistakes come from not confirming the facts," Gus said.

Well, I thought, if nothing else, he sure has those percentages down.

Gus wanted to try to get into Granny Goose's yard again, maybe later in the day, but I nixed that because her gate was still locked and Mom had said Granny Goose would be working the Tarts' tent through the evening. So we planned to meet on the courthouse square for the pancake breakfast at eight o'clock the next morning, then hit Simply Paris at eight twenty-five or so, right before the staff meeting. One of us would be the lookout—probably Margaret because she was the most scared—while the other two scoped out François' office and pantry. I was a little worried the doors would be locked—especially after his blowup this morning—but we'd deal with that if it happened.

It was almost time to get back to work at Mom's

smoothie booth, so we crunched the last of the ice from our lemon shake-ups, tossed the cups, and headed out of the midway. "Are you sure you guys don't have a rehearsal tomorrow morning?" I said.

"Nope," Gus said. "We have a final dress rehearsal at two-thirty right before the performance, but that's it. What about you? You got to work with your mom?"

Ugh. I'd almost forgotten. "Yeah. I have to help set up for the Tarts' fish fry and the finale. But that isn't until noon, so we'll have plenty of time."

"By noon," Gus said with a grin, "we'll be at the cops' station, giving our sworn statements."

Chapter 24
Heartless

After my second shift at Mom's smoothie booth I walked home, still dizzy from all the information we'd gathered. This time yesterday I never would've thought we'd be so close to clearing Granny Goose, nabbing two thieves, and winning that reward. It'd taken some patience to get used to Gus and all his weird NSCCB facts, and if I really was honest with myself, I still felt a little jealous over Margaret's friendship with him. One thing I had to give Gus credit for, though: he sure knew how to analyze evidence. Maybe, if my parents let me, I'd join the Not-So-Clueless Crime Busters, too. Especially since Margaret was so gung ho to sign up.

And I thought, with a grin on my face, I was pretty darn good at this, particularly when it came to discovering clues. Besides the locket and the Pitaya and the Ford medallion, I'd been the one to nab François' weekly planner. "A spectacular find," Gus had said, and he'd been right.

I practically skipped the whole way home, excited and thrilled and . . . well . . . just a little bit terrified about tomorrow morning.

"Lindy, will you pass the potatoes please?" Mom said. She'd just finished telling my dad how helpful I'd been all day. They both were beaming with pride about how I'd handled responsibility at the smoothie booth, so I figured now was a good time to warm up to them again about this band camp thing, just in case the heirlooms had already been sold, or our plans went haywire and we didn't get the reward.

Like Gus said, always have a backup plan.

Before I even hit the main part of my spiel—about how everyone else was going to camp—Mom shook her head. "Nope. Sorry, honey. We can't swing it. We got an estimate on the roof, and it was a lot higher than we'd anticipated. And then we've got the computer, Henry's new glasses . . ." She started counting everything off on her fingers again, like she always does.

"And don't forget my bike," Henry said when she finished. "I need a new one, 'cause today when I was washing mine, the chain came off."

Dad laughed and tousled Henry's hair. "That's something the old man can take care of, buddy. No need to get all worked up over a loose chain."

I headed upstairs later after loading the dishwasher, more determined than ever to pull everything off tomorrow, to earn that reward.

"Mom," Henry yelled from the living room, "can I have the scissors?"

"Scissors? For what?" She sounded skeptical.

"It's a surprise," he said, following her into the kitchen. "You can't see until your birthday on Monday."

Mom's birthday?

On Monday?

Oh, no! I'd totally forgotten. So now I had another critical thing to take care of. I'd have to look for a present tomorrow, maybe from one of the craft vendors at the festival. It made me feel bad, though, because usually I spent way more than two days searching for my mom's present. If I hadn't been so worried about my own problems, such as solving this heirloom theft, I'd already have found her something really cool, like I did every year.

I was listening with half my brain as she lectured Henry about the safety rules regarding scissors—the same rules I'd heard a million times—when I thought about the locket. It might be a good idea to check on it.

I did an about-face on the stairs and headed

outside. The garage door was wide open, just how I'd left it that morning when I'd been looking for a new bag of cat food. I flipped the light switch on and searched for the Grubb's grime remover. It should have been on the second shelf above the washing machine, but I didn't see it.

My heart started tap, tap, tapping into a nervous little dance. I climbed Mom's footstool that was in front of the washer and shuffled through a bunch of bottles on the shelf: motor oil, windshield cleanser, lawn fertilizer. No grime remover.

Okay. Now I had a problem, a severe one. In fact, on a problem scale of 1 to 10, with 10 being the very most severe problem in the world, I'd hit a 9.999.

I tried to stay calm. I even tried the deep-breathing trick my mom had taught me from her yoga class. Except it didn't work, because I could barely suck a trickle of air down my windpipe.

I tried talking myself through the search, using logic:

•It can't possibly be gone. No one ever uses the Grubb's grime remover. I must be looking in the wrong spot.

•I put the locket there myself. Margaret and Gus saw me.

•Stay cool. Don't start screaming or crying or anything, because Mom and Dad will hear you.

Fifteen minutes later, after I'd scoured every inch of every shelf in the garage, after I'd memorized every single cleanser and what it cleaned and what to do in case you swallowed it, I got that same sinking bad-test feeling I'd had earlier over Gus.

I sat on the footstool, resting my chin in my hands. Maybe I was missing something. I needed to think more like the NSC crime busters. How would they—

Wait a minute . . .

The footstool.

Why had the footstool been in front of the wash-ing machine? When I used it yesterday to hide the locket, I'd folded it and put it back by the door, where Mom always stores it.

Someone else, the same person who'd taken the locket, obviously, had used it. But who? If it were Mom or Dad, they would've put it back, and then they would've said something like "What the heck is this locket doing in our garage?"

I thought it over some more, and all of a sudden my knees started knocking together. I knew who'd been in our garage.

Suspect Number One: Leonard Snout.

Of course. It had to be him. Leonard had been walking by our house at the exact same time we'd hidden the locket. He'd probably stood outside and watched us. Aaagh! I wanted to scream. Why, why, why had I left the garage door open that day? How many times in my life had my dad yelled, "Keep that garage door closed, Lindy." A thousand maybe?

So now the locket was gone. And it was all my fault.

I turned the light off and closed the garage door. Not that it mattered anymore; the damage had been done. Leonard had outsmarted us. I wondered if he'd already sold the locket. He might've done so without telling François, like a double-cross deal. If that was the case, we might not get the reward at all, even if we did find the other heirlooms. Which once again meant no band camp for me, no chance to play for the governor.

I walked through the living room and around a fort Henry had built. He'd draped a bunch of sheets over some chairs and hung a sign that said, PRIVAT KEEP OUT OR NOK FRIST. I didn't even bother to yell at him about the box of photos and craft supplies I nearly tripped over.

I dragged myself upstairs, one pathetic step at a time. My flip-flops felt like they weighed ten pounds each.

I called Margaret, then Gus. Neither of them was home. I felt a quick pang in my chest. Were they back at the festival without me, maybe talking about tomorrow's plans, or even checking out the midway, riding the Sizzler?

I went downstairs for a glass of juice but stopped outside the kitchen door when I heard the words "Evelyn Unger."

"She called me earlier," Mom said. "I've never heard her so upset. She says the police are insinuating she had something to do with the Grimstones' robbery."

"You're kidding. I've known Evelyn since I was a kid. She wouldn't swipe a loose grape from the Winn-Dixie. What's up, anyway?" Dad said.

"From what I understand, Mrs. Grimstone is linking the robbery to this last Tuesday. That's the day the Tarts were at her house for François' soufflé demonstration. I tell you, I'm baffled. I guess I'll be getting a visit from the police, too. It sounds like they're going to question everyone who was there."

Dad belted out a laugh. "Does that mean you're a suspect? Should I search the garage for the loot?"

Chapter 25
Low-down and Blue

I gasped, nearly swallowing the gum I'd just stuck in my mouth. I inched closer to the door.

"Me, a suspect?" Mom sounded shocked. "Well, good Lord, I hadn't even considered that. I understood the police were going to question everyone's comings and goings at Mrs. Grimstone's that day." She dropped her voice. "You know, I didn't want to admit this to Evelyn, but the only two people I remember leaving the kitchen were her and François. He had to run out to his car for something. Evelyn never did say where she went."

The dishwasher changed cycles, nearly drowning Mom out. I flattened my ear against the door frame.

"Evelyn's worried to death. She doesn't have the money for an attorney."

"They can't arrest her on circumstantial evidence," Dad said. "Have they even searched her house yet?"

"I'm not sure. All I know is—"

The telephone rang. "I'll get it," I yelled. I ran upstairs, almost tripping over Pixie, and grabbed the hall phone.

When Margaret said, "It's me," I slid to the floor with relief. Finally, someone I could talk to.

"Oh no!" she screamed after I'd laid the news on her. I didn't know which got to her most: the business about Granny Goose being questioned or the lost heirloom. Finally, after calming down a little, she took a deep breath and said, "Are you sure your parents didn't find the locket?"

"If my parents found it, I wouldn't be on the phone with you."

"Yeah, you're right. Your mom would probably ground you for at least ten years."

"I haven't told Gus yet," I said. "And my mom won't let me make calls after nine. I guess I'll wait until tomorrow morning to tell him."

"Oh, I forgot," Margaret said, sounding disappointed. "That's why I called. I have to baby-sit Carrie and Sarah in the morning. My parents are going to Orlando for a couple of hours. They're leaving at eight."

"So you can't go with us to Simply Paris?"

"No. I'm so mad. I'm going to be stuck watching two hours straight of *Scooby-Doo*."

When I finally returned the phone to its cradle, an exasperated sigh hissed its way out of my mouth. Another big setback: no Margaret in the morning. That meant it would be only me and the NSC crime buster of the month.

I grabbed Pixie and a Harry Potter book and curled up on my bed. But no matter how hard I tried, I couldn't concentrate on the problems at Hogwarts. All I could think about were my own problems, which felt way bigger than Harry Potter's. It hardly seemed possible that yesterday morning I'd been looking forward to something as simple as riding the Sizzler. How, in such a short time, had everything gotten so mixed up? And if my hunch about Leonard was true, how would I be able to straighten it out?

I tossed the book aside and opened my flute case. Usually I could lose myself in the scales and exercises and forget everything but the music. But not this time. Nothing could take the worry off losing that locket, not even my second chocolate chip cookie.

Still feeling restless, I wandered downstairs. Mom and Dad had a Scrabble game laid out on the kitchen table. Dad had his nose in the dictionary, and Mom was all hunched over her row of letters. She kept rearranging them. I stood in the doorway, feeling a huge pang of guilt. I wanted to tell them the truth—dump the whole problem on them right then and there—but how could I do that without being grounded forever?

Until now I'd always been totally honest with my parents. Well, except for some of the small stuff, like my run-ins with Angel. Mom and Dad trusted me, too, which had made me kind of proud. Boy. Had I ever messed that up.

Okay, Lindy, I thought. Quit feeling sorry for yourself. The only way to fix things is to catch the thieves.

Chapter 26
A New Day Dawns

I was up by seven-thirty the next morning. I shared a piece of cinnamon toast with Henry, took a quick swig of an orange soda I'd hidden in the refrigerator, and then rushed out the door. I even got away before Mom had a chance to start in with her typical comments about my fashion choices, like "Don't you have any shoes in your closet besides flip-flops, Lindy?" or "Isn't that T-shirt a little worn out, dear?"

It was going to be another scorcher outside. I could tell by the early-morning sun; it glowed over the horizon like a giant pink grapefruit.

When I got downtown, the festival was in full

swing: Tarts flipping pancakes, balloon clowns cranking out hats, and the Cornhuskers Bluegrass Band warming up for a group of cloggers.

I found Gus right away. He already had a tower of pancakes drenched in blueberry syrup. I got some, too, then sat across from him. First, I explained about Margaret's baby-sitting job. Next, I told him the newest on Granny Goose's problems. Last, I took a deep breath and said, "Leonard's got the locket."

Gus's eyes bugged way open. "Wha-wha?" He tried to keep talking, but his mouth was too crammed with pancakes and syrup for me to understand him. He gulped and sputtered and held a pointed finger in the air, like he was trying to say, "Just a minute," but I rushed through my story and suspicions about Leonard without taking a breath. The whole time I talked, Gus stared at me and chewed, and when I finished, he leaned back in his chair and wiped a glob of syrup off his chin.

I felt so stupid, like I should have a flaming red

S branded on each cheek, because hadn't Gus been the one to insist we hide the locket on the top shelf? If I'd only just listened to his NSCCB statistics, we wouldn't be in this situation now.

Gus took a swig of his milk. "Don't feel bad," he said, "'cause, seriously, here's the thing: There's only a forty-five percent chance, tops, of a double cross in cases like this. Odds are way higher that Leonard still has the locket, or it's hidden with the other heirlooms at Simply Paris. So don't worry. We're gonna find all of them."

I didn't have a clue where the NSCCBs dug up all their percentage facts, and none of what Gus just said made any sense to me, but for the first time since I'd discovered the locket was gone, I felt a tad bit—maybe 10 percent—better.

After finishing our pancakes, we headed straight to Simply Paris. The wooden cutout of François stood poised outside the café again this morning, only this time it held a different sign:

BLOOMSBERRIANS: MAKE HASTE.

DELIGHT YOUR BUDS OF TASTE!

JOIN US ON THE MORNING OF SATURDAY, THE 18TH DAY OF JUNE, FOR AN UNSURPASSED FRENCH OMELET BREAK-FAST EXTRAVAGANZA, PRESENTED BY FRANÇOIS POUPPIÈRE OF PARIS. DOORS OPEN AT 9:00 A.M. PRECISELY. NO EARLY BIRDS, PLEASE.

(AN ADDED BONUS: PATRONS WILL BE GREETED AND SEATED BY OUR VERY OWN CUCUMBER PRINCESS.)

PATIO DINING IF WEATHER PERMITS. CUCUMBER FESTIVAL SPECIAL, ONLY $25 PER PERSON.

"Oh, crud," I said, "I can't believe Angel's going to be here."

Gus didn't say anything, but his face paled a little. I silently vowed to ruin the second princess gown if Angel muttered even one word to us this morning.

I pressed my nose against the restaurant window. Servers zipped back and forth like honeybees, carrying long-stemmed glasses and silverware and vases filled with flowers. François stood in the middle of the dining room, his mustache tips curled into perfect Os. His apron was gone today, replaced by a sleek black coat with long tails, a black bow tie, and black pants. His chef's hat seemed even puffier than yesterday's, and it had a swirly black F stitched on the front of it.

I couldn't read François' lips, but it looked like he was firing off instructions. Every few seconds he would clap his hands and point to something, and all the servers would scramble in that direction. A stern-looking woman stood beside him, checking things off in a notebook as he spoke. She towered over him, and except for the chef's hat, they were dressed exactly alike. Her raven black hair was pulled into a knot at the back of her neck.

When the woman pointed at a clock on the wall, which read eight twenty-eight, François clapped his hands again. He headed toward the far end of the restaurant, which opened into a large patio. Like robots, the workers all followed him outdoors.

"Man, this is working out perfect," Gus said. "The meeting's supposed to last until eight forty-five. We should be able to scope out the pantry and his office without any problems."

I felt shaky and light-headed as we swept around the alley corner. We strode together toward the kitchen, and just like yesterday, accordion music blared from inside. I pressed my face against the screen door. Gus was right. Not a soul in sight; they all were at the meeting.

Gus looked over his shoulder and down the alley, both ways. "Let's hit it," he said. He pushed on the door.

It didn't open.

Chapter 27

Countdown to Trouble

"It's stuck," Gus muttered. He rammed the frame with the palm of his hand. The door flew open, slamming into a tall coatrack. The rack crashed to the floor, and a bunch of white aprons and chef hats sailed across the kitchen.

We scurried around the floor like mice after crumbs, trying to get everything picked up and hung back on the rack. The wall clock read eight thirty-two. We'd already blown two minutes.

I checked out the tidy kitchen. Sauces simmered on a twelve-burner stove; chopped veggies sat in bowls, waiting for their omelets; and long loaves of French bread—at least twenty of them—were lined up on the counter. Next to me, a collection of knives glistened against the wall: long, skinny fish knives; short paring knives; bread knives; curved knives; hooked knives; serrated knives. It was the knife in the middle that raised the hairs on my neck: bigger than a hatchet, with a razor-sharp edge. I shivered. What did François use that for anyway?

We crossed the kitchen and ventured into a narrow hallway. Three closed doors led off it. The door to my right had a sign that said EMPLOYEES' RESTROOM, so we could scratch that. The door to my left was unmarked. Gus turned the knob. "It's the pantry," he said. "I'll take it. You take the office."

He pointed down the hall to a door with frosted glass. I approached it cautiously. A wooden plaque on the wall said, CHEF'S OFFICE. KNOCK BEFORE ENTERING!

"Wait," I whispered. "What if someone comes back here? Let's go over our escape plan."

"Okay, if one of us hears or sees something, we'll cough three times to let the other know. Then, when the coast is clear, we'll take off back through the kitchen. Got it?"

I nodded, but my heart hammered hard. I still hadn't forgotten François' meltdown from yesterday.

Gus stepped into the pantry, then peeked back out at me. "This might take awhile. There's a bunch of stuff stored in here," he said. "I'll meet you in the alley at eight forty-five."

And then he disappeared, pulling the door after him.

Now it was my turn. I reached for the knob, my hand so slick with sweat I could barely turn it. Luckily, it opened. I flipped the overhead light on and slipped into the room, closing the door after me. Where to begin?

The first thing I checked was a large wooden desk in the corner. It was crammed with framed photographs of François, loose papers, recipe books, and garden catalogs. A cutlery magazine was opened to page 16, where the headline read, No Matter How You Slice It, the Knife Makes the Difference.

A digital clock on François' desk said 8:35. Ten minutes until the meeting ended. I wasn't having any luck on top of the desk; maybe I should look under it. I leaned down, checked all around the floor. Nothing. Just an empty trash can. I started to pull myself up, then . . .

Rrrrrring . . . rrrrrring . . . rrrrrring.

The phone! Suppose François ran in here to answer it? Panicking, I scrambled under the desk. I scooted as far back as possible and huddled against the trash can.

The phone rang five times, until François' answering machine picked up. "*Bonjour.* You have contacted the office of Chef François Pouppière, proprietor of Simply Paris, European dining at its best. Deliver a message, *s'il vous plaît*, and I shall return it as quickly as possible. *Merci beaucoup.*"

"Yeah, uh . . . hello," said the caller. "Snout here."

Leonard! I almost spit up in the trash can, his voice scared me so bad.

"I'll be over today at four with everything," he said, "after you close shop. Got the rest of those Pitayas—that ruby variety you liked." He chuckled, sending shivers up my spine. "So, errr . . . guess we'll go over everything you've got before your trip, eh? Oh, one last thing. My labor's gonna run higher than the original estimate."

You could've knocked me over with a puff of air. Leonard and François, today at four, and Leonard was bringing the Pitayas. The locket, too, I bet. And I'd been lucky enough to hear all about it.

Wait till I told Gus and Margaret. They'd flip.

I crawled out from under the desk, all set to run to the pantry after Gus. But when I stood up, I noticed a door in the far corner.

Could more of the heirlooms be in there?

François was hiding some of them, I'd just heard so. "Guess we'll go over everything *you've* got," Leonard had said.

I checked the clock again. Six minutes, plenty of time. I sped across the floor and opened the door, into a closet. Against the back wall sat some kind of bundle, covered with a blanket. I dropped to my knees, lifted the blanket, and pulled out a small suitcase.

I fumbled with the clasps. Locked. I shook it. Whatever was in there rattled and slid around like . . . *jewelry!*

I'd found the heirlooms.

I leaped up from the floor, ready to shout, "Hallelujah!" I reached for the suitcase. Should I take it? No, bad idea. Because it wasn't holding all the heirlooms; Leonard still had the Pitayas and the locket. If I took the suitcase and François checked the closet later, he'd tip Leonard off. We might not recover everything.

We'd have to wait until four o'clock when they met, when they had everything laid out. I pushed the suitcase into the closet, threw the blanket over it, then flew across the room. I turned off the light and slipped back into the hallway, trembling with excitement.

I'd just started after Gus when footsteps clicked across the kitchen floor. Snappy, no-nonsense clicks, and they were getting louder.

Chapter 28
Impostor!

I stood against the hallway wall, frozen with fright. I couldn't yell for Gus. I'd be heard. There wasn't time to run to the pantry after him; it was too close to the kitchen. So I coughed. Three huge hacking barks that left my throat raw.

"Goodness. That's quite a cough, dear. Allergies?"

I spun around. A woman—the same one who'd been with François in the dining room—stood a millimeter away from the pantry door. She looked at me curiously. Could she hear my heart, thumping its way up my throat?

"Er . . . I'm fine, thanks." I sputtered one last,

pathetic cough into my fist. What was Gus doing? I hoped he'd heard my warning, and that he'd stay hidden.

"My goodness," she said, "I certainly didn't expect to find our Princess in the bowels of the restaurant."

Princess? Oh, no. She thought I was Angel.

"I'm Greta, François' fiancée." She grasped my hand firmly, pumping my arm like it was a barbell. "I run the dining room, so you'll be reporting to me. Now. First things first. Let's take care of that cough." She took my arm, and I obediently pattered beside her to the kitchen, every nerve in my body on fire.

Greta poured a tall glass of water and handed it to me. I took a swig, then another and another, frantically thinking of something to say.

"Th-thank you."

"Are you certain you'll be able to greet properly? François will have a fit if you cough on any of our diners." She had her back to me and was flipping through the rack of aprons and hats.

"This should do nicely." She pulled a miniature chef's hat from the rack and tugged it onto my head. "Although we definitely need to do something with those bangs."

She tucked my loose hair under the hat, then stepped back and studied me, frowning. "No," she said, crinkling her nose. "The shorts and flip-flops are not going to work. Actually, I'm a bit taken aback by your attire. François and I expected you to arrive in your princess gown."

"Sorry. It's stained."

"Tsk, tsk, that's a shame." She grabbed a long white apron and pulled it over my neck, wrapping its strings around and around my waist, tying them so tight I could barely breathe. "This will have to do. At least it will hide the shorts. Okay, dear, let's go. The doors open soon. It's about time for you to charm our customers."

She took my arm, and I forced three more coughs up from my lungs, signaling to Gus the coast was clear. I hoped he heard me.

I clunked alongside Greta, sweating like my dad after a hard day at the fire station. What would happen when the real Princess showed up? Or even worse, what if François recognized me? He'd peg me as an impostor right away. Did he know I had the planner? Suppose Cricket had told him I'd been in his car?

I looked around, plotting my escape. I'd have to slip back through the kitchen, but I couldn't go anywhere until Greta left my side.

"I'll let François know you're here in a minute," she said. "First, I want to go over your routine."

She took hold of my shoulders. "Stand up straight, please. As you well know from your beauty pageant experience, posture is a critical component of poise. Do . . . not . . . slouch. I repeat, do not slouch!"

I snapped my shoulders back and stood at attention, straighter than a bamboo rod. No point in getting her irritated with me now. If we got this over with quick, maybe she'd join François on the patio and I could get away before Angel showed up.

"You are the official greeter," she explained. "The first impression of Simply Paris, so to speak. Do you comprehend that?"

"Uh . . . yes."

"Good. Now, we'd like to see your Princess qualities shine through to our diners. Do you know how to curtsy?"

"Uh, well . . ."

Uh-oh. From the corner of my eye, I'd just spotted trouble, all decked out in a pink gown. She was standing outside the restaurant door with her grandmother. Mrs. Grimstone rapped on the glass.

"Hold on," Greta said to me. "We've got early birds. You know, I'm sometimes astounded at the rudeness of people. The sign clearly states that we open at nine. Can't they read?"

She clicked across the granite floor, toward the door.

The last thing I saw before running was Gus. He

was standing behind Mrs. Grimstone, waving at me.

Once I made it to the kitchen I tore off the apron and the hat and flew out the back door. I shot down the alley, trying to swallow the squeal at the back of my throat. I slid to a stop where the alley met the sidewalk, then peeked around the corner. Gus was still staring in the window of Simply Paris, looking confused.

I couldn't go get him, because I couldn't chance being seen outside the café's window by Greta. Suppose she pointed me out to Mrs. Grimstone, saying, "This girl is an impostor! Someone call her mother immediately."

I whistled, and Gus looked up. I whistled again, caught his eye for a split second, then ducked back into the alley.

"Oh, man," he said, swinging around the corner of the building to join me. "That was a close call."

"You're telling me." I leaned against the brick wall, still shaking. And then I filled him in on what

I'd found and overheard in François' office.

"Holy tamale! That's awesome! I can't believe it!" He sputtered on and on, praising me so much I thought I'd burst with pride. "Man," he said, "this is one hundred percent in the bag now. All we have to do is be here for the four o'clock meeting."

"Sounds good to me." I grinned at him, but on the inside I was still shivering. What if Leonard and François caught us? They wouldn't be exactly thrilled about three kids foiling their plans. I'd already gotten an earful of François' temper, and Leonard wasn't what you would call a fluffy little teddy bear.

I started down the alley, anxious to get away from Simply Paris before Greta or François saw me, maybe go for a cold drink and work up more nerve for this four o'clock rendezvous. Gus called me back. "Wait. I almost forgot. I just overheard Mrs. Grimstone tell her husband she wanted to talk to Cricket. She mentioned Granny Goose, and it sounds like something else happened. Maybe you should go in the salon, see if you can get the scoop."

"Me?" I wasn't so sure I could pull it off, the way my heart was still pounding.

"Yeah. I'd go, but I figured it'd look funny for a guy to be hanging around a hair salon. Know what I mean?"

I said, "Okay," and Gus waited in the alley while I hurried past the front window of Simply Paris. Opening the door to Shear Magic, I quickly checked out the salon, looking for Cricket and Mrs. Grimstone. I didn't see them, so I figured they must be somewhere in the back, behind the row of whirring hair dryers.

The girl behind the counter clipped on her MARCY name tag and looked up at me. "You here for a trim?" she said, staring at my bangs. She rapped her fingers on the appointment book.

"Oh. Hi, Marcy. I, uh, would like to schedule a haircut. How about next week?"

"Yeah, but I only got an opening with Tammi. Chenille, Deb, Paula, and Madison are booked up, and Cricket's going to be out of town for the next couple of weeks. I've got Wednesday at ten."

"That'll work fine," I said over my shoulder as I headed to the far end of the salon. "I'll be right back. I just need to use your bathroom." I wound my way around the dryers and comb-out stations, stopping in front of a curtain with a sign that said NEW NAILS NOW! MANICURES/PEDICURES. When I heard Mrs. Grimstone's voice behind the curtain, I parted it, ever so slightly.

"There should be an arrest very soon," Mrs. Grimstone said to Cricket. "I just stopped by the police station. An officer was at the Unger woman's house this morning, and of all things, he found one of my Pitayas in that kook's turtle pen."

Chapter 29
Getting to Know Gus

Cricket looked up from the pedicure table where she was arranging nail polish. I have to say, she seemed as surprised as I was. "Oh, my God! Are you sure it's your egg?"

"Certainly it's my egg," Mrs. Grimstone said. "I've examined it thoroughly. It's one of only six Pitayas of its kind, all of them stolen from me on Tuesday. Let me tell you, I'm absolutely over the moon about this recovery. Of course it needs to be cleaned. What a sight. Turtle droppings all over it. I'll have Howard take it to my jeweler."

Cricket mumbled as though she were talking to

herself. "I can't believe it. They found it in the crazy woman's *turtle* pen?"

I checked over my shoulder to make sure no one was watching before opening the curtain a hair wider.

"Are you not feeling well, Cricket?" Mrs. Grimstone said. "Honestly, you look white as a ghost."

"Oh, I'm fine. Just completely shocked, you know, to think a thief is living two doors down from me. But yeah, this is fantastic news. Did they find all the heirlooms at the goose lady's?"

"No, and that's the problem," Mrs. Grimstone said. "Evidently—and this is to go no farther than these four walls, as the police don't want it out yet— she's denying any involvement. Can you imagine? They caught her red-handed. Now didn't I insist all along that woman was behind this? That's *exactly* what I told Howard. I said, 'Howard, that goose nut has something to do with this.'"

"Sounds like she's your thief, all right," Cricket said. "Where do you suppose the police will go from here?"

They better go straight next door to Simply Paris, I wanted to yell, because that's where the real perp is. Instead, I bit my tongue and opened the curtain wider.

"I haven't the faintest notion," Mrs. Grimstone said. She leaned toward a mirror on the wall, picking something off her lip. "I certainly hope she confesses soon. I'm desperate to have those pieces returned."

I closed the curtain and eased my way toward the front door.

"You won't believe what's happened," I said when I joined Gus in the alley.

After I told him, he shook his head, looking disappointed. "Man, I wish we could've gotten back in her yard and hidden that egg. The only thing we can do now is make sure this afternoon's plan is one hundred percent foolproof."

We headed back to the festival midway where we lost at a bunch of dart games, ate more kettle corn, and rode the Sizzler three times. We even talked about stuff that didn't have anything to do with heirlooms or perps or NSCCB, like school and Gus's funny French relatives. He cracked me up with some of the stories he told.

Then we started talking about concert band and how much fun camp was going to be. "I really want to get picked for the governor's concert," he said, "but I doubt if I do. I'm not near as good a musician as you." I felt my face turn pink. Gosh, if I was good enough for Gus to notice, maybe I did have a chance of playing for the governor.

"Aw, you'll probably get picked," I said, trying to build up his confidence a little, but truthfully, I wasn't all that sure about those odds. I'd never heard anyone squeak so much on an instrument as Gus.

"I wish it was you playing in the finale trio today," he said. "You're way better than Angel—nicer, too. I can hardly stand practicing with her. All she does is criticize me."

We bought curly fries and killed more time shooting darts at the midway, and then I remembered Mom's birthday. "Let's go to the craft tents.

I've got to find something for my mom."

We sped by the tents with quilts and lawn orna-
ments, heading straight for the jewelry. Gus helped
me pick out a tiny pair of earrings from a Native
American vendor. "These are way cool," he said.
"Turquoise. My mom always liked turquoise."

He turned his head, but I'd seen that his eyes were
glistening. All of a sudden my heart hurt for Gus—for
the loneliness he must've felt every single night, when it
was just him and his memories and that big dark sky.

I traced a figure eight in the sand with the toe of my
flip-flop. "I bet your mom looked really pretty in turquoise, you know, with her dark hair and everything."

"Yeah," he said. "She did."

I paid for the earrings and tucked them safely
down in my pocket, thinking how they were double
extra special, in honor of two great mothers—Gus's
and mine. "Thanks for helping pick these out," I said.
"My mom's going to love them."

By then I'd spent every last cent of my money,

so Gus bought both our sodas. I checked his watch. Eleven: time to call Margaret. I found a pay phone outside the courthouse.

Luckily, her parents had just gotten home and she was off the hook from baby-sitting. "We'll meet you by the bingo tent," I said.

"Did you find the you-know-what?" she whispered.

"No, but we've got lots to tell you."

"Like what? You're getting along okay with Gus, aren't you?"

"Yeah. You were right. He really is funny. Nice, too."

"What all did you do?" she said, and I thought I detected a hint of something familiar—jealousy maybe?—in her voice.

"I can't go into it now, but it's big."

"Gosh. That's not fair. I can't believe I got stuck home with the twins while you guys had all the fun."

I didn't say it, but I was thinking that it hadn't been exactly a barrel of laughs when I'd nearly gotten busted as an impostor. "Just hurry up and get down here, okay?"

She made it in five minutes, and she oohed and aahed and held her hand over her mouth while Gus and I told her everything that'd happened, but I seriously thought she was going to have a heart attack when we got to the part about the egg and Granny Goose.

"Oh . . . no." She clutched her chest, the color draining from her face. "We've got to get over to her house and see what's happening. At least we can help out with the animals or something."

Gus and I agreed to go along, but truthfully, I worried Granny Goose wouldn't even be there, that she'd already been fingerprinted and booked at the Bloomsberry police station. Or what if the cops were tearing through her house at this very moment, searching for the rest of the heirlooms?

Chapter 30
Poor Pitiful Pickles

On our walk across town we went over our strategy for the four o'clock meeting between Leonard and François. "We'll get there early," Gus said, "and wait in the alley for—"

"Wait a minute," Margaret said. "We've got that stupid finale. Mr. Austin said our trio will start around three-fifteen."

Gus shrugged. "No problem. We'll be done way before four."

"I think two of us should sneak in the kitchen door again," I said. "And then one of us"—probably Margaret, because she was still the most scared—

"can stay outside, in case of an emergency."

"Right," Gus said. "If they meet in François' office, we'll eavesdrop outside the door. Since the café's closing for patio work, I bet no one else will be there."

I stopped on the sidewalk. "What if François' fiancée, Greta, is there? That'll mess everything up."

Gus shook his head. "Nah, no way she's involved. There's less than a thirty percent chance he'd tell his fiancée he's a crook."

"Okay," Margaret said. "So what happens if they meet on the patio, instead of in the office?"

"You can watch through the fence posts. Lindy and I'll try to get a good view of them from the inside, maybe find a window that looks out onto the patio," Gus said. "I'll have my dad's cell. As soon as we get some proof, either by hearing something or photos, it's a quick nine-one-one."

He seemed to think our upcoming rendezvous would play out like a first-grade math problem, and I went along with him, acting all brave about everything. Deep down, though, I wasn't so sure. I couldn't put my finger on it, but all of a sudden I had this nagging worry that something might go wrong. Something big.

I tried to ignore my growing doubts as Margaret and I headed up Granny Goose's porch steps. Margaret rang the doorbell, and just like the last time, we didn't get an answer. I peeked inside the window again. Other than Doris the duck, nestled on the couch, there wasn't any sign of activity.

Gus ran around from the side of the house and joined us on the porch. "The backyard gate's locked," he said. "They must have her down at headquarters."

"Oh, this is so awful," Margaret said. "And unfair, too. I can't believe they're arresting an innocent person. What about Pickles? Who's going to take care of her? She needs lots of attention, you know. She's just a helpless animal."

"I bet Granny Goose called her son to help," I said, trying to make Margaret feel better. "I remember her saying he lives in Orlando. He's a veterinarian."

That calmed her down a little, and we'd just decided to leave when we heard the honk. It came from the direction of Cricket's house.

Margaret snapped her head around. "That's Pickles."

"AAAGH! GET BACK! GET AWAY FROM ME, YOU—YOU BEAST!"

"Hold on!" Margaret shouted. She flew down the steps and across the lawn toward Cricket's, yelling the whole way, "Don't worry, I'll get her. Here, Pickles, Pickles. Here, good girl."

By the time Gus and I made it to Cricket's yard, Margaret already had Pickles scooped into her arms. "Wittle bitty baby was scared, wasn't her?" she cooed. "But don't you worry one wittle bit, 'cause Auntie Margo's gonna take care of you."

Pickles bobbed her neck and made some kind of weird, gargling sound. Her leash hung from the harness around her body, and a shiny, SureFresh mint tin was clamped in her bill.

Cricket stood by a small storage shed at the side of her house, clutching a Shear Magic duffel bag against her chest. She jabbed her finger at Pickles. "Oh, my God. That hideous thing nearly pecked my eyes out. I was in my shed getting supplies when it flew at me from out of nowhere. It got my mints."

I worked the SureFresh tin out of Pickles's mouth and handed it to Cricket. "Sorry about that. She likes shiny stuff."

"I don't care what she likes. Just get her away from me—*now!*" She took a couple of deep breaths, eyeing me with a "what are you doing back here" kind of expression. "Snooping again—after our little talk? I thought we had an understanding. I have your mom's number at the shop, you know."

"Oh, we're absolutely not snoopers," Margaret said. "We just stopped by to visit Mrs. Unger, but she's not home. You don't happen to know where she is, do you?"

"I've got a pretty good idea, but I'm not at liberty to say." Cricket headed toward the front of her house, calling over her shoulder, "Make sure that goose stays out of my yard."

I patted Pickles on the head as we left Cricket's. "What are we supposed to do with her now? Granny Goose is gone, maybe in jail"—Margaret winced when I said that—"and Pickles is locked out of the yard."

"We'll take her with us," Margaret said. "She's a good goose, aren't you, Pickles? She has her leash on, so she won't get lost." Pickles paced back and forth between us, bobbing her head and making soft, gurgling noises. I couldn't help feeling sorry for her, especially since she might not have a home much longer.

I thought maybe I should prepare Margaret for the worst. "You know, Granny Goose might not come home tonight. What do you want to do about Pickles if that happens?"

"She'll spend the night at my house. Won't you, baby?"

"Suppose Granny Goose is gone, you know, like more than a night? Like, maybe, for way more than a night."

Margaret's chin jutted out. "I'll keep her for good then. I'll take Doris the duck, too."

Chapter 31
Preparations . . .

I checked Gus's watch as soon as we got back to the courthouse square. Eleven-fifty. I was due at the Tarts' tent at noon to help set up for the afternoon fish fry and the festival finale. I couldn't chance being late and irritating my mom; otherwise, she might nix my plans for the rest of the day.

Gus called Granny Goose's from the courthouse pay phone. He left a message on her machine that we had Pickles, and then we met my mom at twelve on the dot.

"This is a feather in your cap, Miss Lindy," Mom said, smiling. "Right on time. I guess you haven't been up to anything too outrageous today. And would one of you like to tell me why you have Evelyn's goose?"

"We're helping Mrs. Unger out this afternoon," Margaret said, patting Pickles's head.

"Well, I guess that explains it then." From the way Mom smiled, I figured she hadn't heard the latest on Granny Goose.

She gave me detailed instructions for the setup: "don't do this," and "be sure to do that," and "don't leave before you do this." It sounded like I'd be busy for hours.

Margaret and Gus offered to help. "We have to leave for our instruments around two, though," Margaret said. "Remember, we have that dress rehearsal before the finale."

She looked over her shoulder at Gus, then mouthed to me, "Squeaking problem."

I didn't doubt that one bit.

The four of us, counting Pickles, who was practically attached to Margaret at the hip by now, arranged tables and chairs and hung banners. We went over our plans, too. Gus kept assuring Margaret and me that everything would work out fine. "It'll be so cool," he said. "I can't wait to see the looks on those guys' faces when they get nabbed."

We were taking a lunch break when Mr. Austin stopped by our table.

"Glad I found you," he said. And then he put one arm around Gus and the other around Margaret, which of course didn't leave an arm for me. "You two haven't forgotten about your performance with Angel today, have you?"

"We haven't forgotten," Margaret said. "Court-house at two-thirty for the practice, right?"

"Uh, excuse me, Mr. Austin," I said. "We have a little something to do at around three forty-five. You think they'll be finished by then?"

He pulled a schedule out of his back pocket. "Let's see. The tap dancers are on at three-thirty, and the trio is right before that, so it looks as if your friends will be good to go in plenty of time."

"How come you have to leave so early, Lindy?" trilled a snooty voice from behind me. "Do you have a date?" Angel scooted up beside Mr. Austin. She had on the same pink princess gown as this morning, and she was swinging a sleek, shiny flute at her side. Angel flashed the flute in my face, smirking like Pixie after she's polished off a can of tuna. "Grammy had it sent from Germany. They make superexpensive flutes over there, you know."

Germany Schmermany. I stuffed a handful of potato chips in my mouth.

"It's very nice, Angel," Mr. Austin said, smiling at her. "Okay, Gus. I'll see you and Margaret at practice. Make sure you have a good reed."

"Oh. Uh, yeah. No problem. I've got a couple of new ones in my case."

"Great. See you later." Mr. Austin took off across the lawn.

As soon as he was gone, Angel leaned into her friend Caroline's ear. "Mr. Austin forgot to tell the sexy-phone player to bring two hundred sets of ear-plugs," she said in a fake whisper. "Because the audience is going to need them once he starts squeaking."

"Oh, yeah? Well they're going to need heavy-duty nose plugs when you play. Because you totally stink," I said.

"Shut . . . up. The only thing that stinks around here is you," Angel said, "and that stupid goose."

Okay, that did it. She didn't need to go insulting an innocent animal. I brushed a piece of shortcake off the table, next to the Princess's foot, then snapped my fingers and tugged at Pickles's leash. Like a cyclone, she blew out from under the table and went straight for Angel's ankles.

Gus, Margaret, and I cracked up laughing as the Princess ran across the lawn, screaming her head off.

After we'd finished eating, the three of us dragged more chairs from the courthouse, lining them in rows for the festival finale. It seemed like everyone in Bloomsberry but me would be performing today:

ballet dancers, baton twirlers, the Cucumber Jazz Quartet. Even the Senior Squares were scheduled for a line dance.

At two, Gus and Margaret left for their instruments so they could make it back in time for their final rehearsal. When they raced across the lawn with Pickles, jealousy poked at my chest like an icicle. Once again they were doing something without me. I straightened rows of chairs, helped Mom set out condiments, and sliced cucumbers for the salad.

The whole time I worked I tried to forget about not being a part of the trio. I tried not to be resentful of Angel, who was playing *my* part in *my* favorite concert piece with *my* friends. Instead, I focused on the upcoming rendezvous. I kept reminding myself that in just a few hours the three of us would be way more than a small festival act. We'd be town heroes. We'd be rich. And I'd have a chance to play in a way more important concert—that one in Tallahassee.

Chapter 32
Henry's Heavy Heart

My mom sent me home around three to feed Pixie, give Dad her last-minute shopping list of things she needed for the fish fry, and walk Henry back to the festival.

I set the bag with Mom's earrings on a bookshelf and gave Dad his grocery list. He grumbled a little about "Why didn't we get these supplies all taken care of yesterday when we were at Winn-Dixie?" He found his keys and his wallet and took off.

After pouring Pixie a bowl of salmon nuggets, I headed upstairs for Henry. He was in his room, hiding under another blanket fort. Wrapping paper, ribbons, and tape were strewn across the floor.

"You're going to get in big trouble if you don't clean that mess up quick," I yelled on my way to the bathroom. "Mom's going to be really mad if you leave it."

The kitchen clock had read three-oh-five. I had ten minutes to get back to the festival and watch Margaret and Gus perform. Only forty-five minutes until we were in the alley behind Simply Paris. I tried to forget my nagging worry about things going wrong. Instead, I focused on the reward that awaited us.

Hopefully, we'd have everything wrapped up by five this afternoon. We'd still have time to eat at the fish fry, maybe even ride the Sizzler again. And then we'd be on the front page of tomorrow's paper.

I couldn't wait to see the look on Angel's face when I swaggered up to the front of City Hall and collected our five thousand dollars. She was going to have a cow.

I poked my head back in Henry's room. He hadn't

picked up the first thing. "Come on," I said. "Quit wasting time."

He crawled out from his tent, holding a fistful of wrapping paper. "I'm not wasting time. I'm wrapping Mom's present. And ha, ha, ha. It's going to be way better than what you got her. Look. See if you can guess what it is."

When he handed me a small, heavy, heart-shaped object wrapped in Christmas paper . . . well, let's just say my own heart screamed "Cardiac arrest!" Now I'm not psychic or anything. But I knew, after eyeing the mess on his floor, what was inside the Santa Claus paper.

Old pictures, cut in heart-shaped designs, were strewn everywhere. And, it occurred to me that Henry said he'd cleaned his bike yesterday. Okay. Cleaned it with what? I'd be willing to bet the whole five-thousand-dollar reward he'd used Grubb's grime remover.

I shook his present and tried to act casual. "Cool. Can I see what's inside it?"

"No. It's a secret."

"Pretty please with sugar on it, and I'll give you my Boggle Junior and Scrabble Kids game."

He made pouty lips. His forehead crinkled, like he was deep in thought, like this negotiation equaled a baseball card trade. "I don't want the Boggle Junior or Scrabble Kids."

"What do you want?" *Little brat.*

"Your soccer ball. You know, the one that famous player signed."

Drat. Now why'd he have to go and ask for that, my all-time favorite collector item? Henry didn't even play soccer. He was a T-ball fanatic.

"No."

"You can't see it, then." He grabbed the present from me and tucked it neatly into his pocket.

"Okay, okay. You can have the soccer ball. Just give me the present."

"Go get the ball first."

Grrrr. Thwarted again. I wanted to shake him till his baby teeth rattled loose, but that would take too much time. His Mickey Mouse clock read three-twelve. I flew to my room, then back with the soccer ball.

Henry snatched it and ran downstairs. "Ha-ha, tricked ya!" he yelled.

I raced down the stairs after him, and tackled him before he got out the front door. The scuffle didn't last long, because I was dead set on getting that present. After worming it out of his pocket, I tore off the wrapper.

Yep. It was the locket all right. I flicked the clasp open.

Oh.

Crud.

Angel's picture was gone. It'd been replaced by a photo of Henry and me in our bathing suits at the beach.

It took me three whole minutes to convince Henry we couldn't keep the locket because I'd found it outside Quick Mart and had to return it. It took two minutes to locate the original picture of the

Princess. It took one minute to bust open my piggy bank and hand him every cent I owned. All in all, I lost six minutes and $12.15.

"They have lockets at Dino's Dollar Store," I promised Henry. "Later today Dad can drive you over there, and you can buy Mom one that's a lot prettier than this ugly thing."

"Yeah," he sniffled. "But are they gold?"

"Oh, yes," I fibbed. "Solid gold." Well, actually it wasn't too big of a fib, because I had seen gold heart-shaped lockets once at Dino's Dollar. They were gaudy, but at least they were affordable. Henry would probably be able to buy two lockets and have money left over for perfume.

He stopped whining, finally, when I promised he could help me bake Mom a chocolate birthday cake. We left the house at three-nineteen. I had the locket in one pocket and Angel's picture in the other.

I nearly pulled Henry's arm out of its socket as I dragged him to the square. "Remember," I whispered before dropping him off with Mom, "you can't say one single word about this locket. It's our special secret. If you say anything, you're going to get grounded for the whole summer for getting into Dad's grime remover, because it's *dangerous poison*, and you're not allowed to touch it. You won't be able to play T-ball or anything. And I'll take the soccer ball back."

"Gotta go," I said to Mom after giving Henry one last secret Look.

"I don't know what your rush is," she said. "They're having problems with the loudspeaker system. Margaret and Gus won't be onstage for a good while."

"What?" My jaw dropped. We were supposed to be on our way to Simply Paris in a few minutes.

I must've looked like I'd just seen a spaceship or something, because Mom's eyes widened with her superconcerned expression. She felt my forehead. "Are you all right, Lindy? You feel a little warm. And honestly, your face has lost its color."

She crossed her arms over her chest. "Wait a minute. Have you had anything substantial to eat today, or has it all been sugar, sugar, sugar?"

"It's been all sugar, sugar, sugar," Henry said. "I saw her with an orange soda this morning."

"Soda? In the morning? For goodness' sake, Lindy. You know better than that."

"I just had a couple of sips, honest." I backed away from her, glancing over my shoulder at the stage. No sign of any performance activity, but I did see several men gathered around one of the speakers. "It looks like they're fixing things," I said. "Guess I'll run over and watch the concert."

"Make sure you eat some fish later," Mom called out. "You need the protein."

I hurried to the crowded stage area, searching for Margaret and Gus. I figured they had to be around somewhere, because Pickles was tied to a front-row chair.

"Over here, Lindy," Margaret called. She and Gus were on the far side of the stage, surrounded by a troupe of kindergarten tap dancers.

"What's going on?" I yelled after pushing my way through the crowd. "We're going to be late."

"We've got a problem," Gus shouted from the stage. I could barely see him or Margaret for all the screaming tap dancers.

"The sound system broke down," Margaret said. "Everything's running behind."

Great. Just great. I couldn't even tell them about finding the locket, because they were up onstage, and I was down in the audience, and there were a million people swarming all around and between us, ranting about the broken sound system.

"Good news!" someone yelled over my shoulder. "Looks like everything's been fixed. Someone try the mike."

The next thing I knew the Princess had the microphone, acting like some big shot stage manager. "Testing. One, two, three. Testing. One, two, three."

Gus broke free of the tap dancers and made his

way to the edge of the stage. He leaned over so I could hear him. "Here's the thing. There's only two acts in front of us, so—"

"Hey you!" Angel's voice blared from the speakers. "Gus Kinnard. Quit talking to your girlfriend and get behind the curtain."

Gus rolled his eyes and kept whispering. "Go on to Simply Paris, okay? But don't go in the patio by yourself or anything; it's too dangerous. Just keep an eye out and wait for us. We'll dump the instruments and be over there as quickly as possible. Fifteen minutes, max."

"Psst, Lindy!" Margaret hissed from behind him. Her eyes looked big with worry. "Be careful. Don't let them see you."

"Ahem." Mr. Austin cleared his throat from the far side of the stage. "Let's go, Gus and Margaret. Backstage, please."

So now it was up to me—all by myself—to start the perp patrol at Simply Paris.

Chapter 33

The Rendezvous

According to the courthouse clock, I had ten minutes before the meeting at François' café. So I didn't exactly have time to stand around feeling sorry for myself because I'd lost my partners. I took off across the lawn, turned onto Orange Blossom Avenue, and followed it until I was standing across the street from Simply Paris. A sign on the door said, CLOSED THROUGH JULY 4TH FOR PATIO RENOVATIONS.

I couldn't chance running into François outside his kitchen, so I circled the block until I found the alley that ran behind the patio. There wasn't a soul in sight, not even a delivery truck. I stood at the alley entrance, swatting gnats from my face, trying to gather my nerve. The sun sizzled overhead like an electrified lemon, singeing my feet to the ground, frying every thought that crossed my mind.

Simply Paris sat five buildings down on the left. I swallowed a gulp and started toward it, one cautious step at a time, as if I were playing hide-and-seek with a pack of alley cats.

When I reached Shear Magic, I peeked through the salon's back door window. The hairdressers must've left early to watch the festival finale because all the lights were out. Good. At least I wouldn't run into Cricket again.

I edged toward the corner of François' patio. The sudden crunch of tires over gravel stopped me cold. Uh-oh! Someone had turned into the alley from behind me. I ducked into a dark, narrow space between the patio and Shear Magic. I'd barely gotten situated behind a cluster of ivy before Leonard's rusty pickup truck rattled by. It pulled into the parking lot on the other side of the alley.

Leonard got out of the truck, holding a Winn-Dixie bag. The Pitayas!

I squished deeper into my hiding nook and watched him cross the alley. He pushed on the wrought-iron gate, but it didn't open. He looked around, then punched a button by the Simply Paris sign on the fence.

Bzzzz!

I peeked around the ivy. Leonard set the bag down. He shuffled his feet impatiently, then jabbed the button again, three times, like he was poking someone in the chest.

Bzzzz! Bzzzz! Bzzzz!

"*Oui, oui,*" called François from inside the patio. "I am coming. Patience, *s'il vous plaît.* No need to fatigue the buzzer, my friend."

I heard a scuttling across the patio. The gate swung open.

"Hello, hello, and a fabulous day to you, *monsieur,*" François sang out. Gosh. His cheeriness surprised me. For someone who was pulling off a million-dollar heist, he didn't sound the least bit nervous.

Leonard muttered something, then picked up the bag and disappeared through the gate. Now I could barely hear them, and I couldn't see through the iron posts of the fence because it was so thick with ivy and honeysuckle. I'd have to move closer. I crept toward the gate, stopping just short of it. It hung open by a millimeter.

I caught a glimpse of François' white hat, bobbing up and down as he spoke. "Pay close attention, please, *monsieur,*" he said. "I shall review my diagram with you in great detail."

A diagram? Since when did you need a diagram to talk about stolen heirlooms?

"Well now," François said. "First things firstly. I do hope you have procured the tools we will need for this endeavor, as I have nothing to offer but fillet knives and meat cleavers." He laughed—a high-pitched trill that made my skin crawl—then said, "But you, my friend, are aware of that, *n'est-ce pas?* Any questions, sir?"

"Yeah," Leonard said, "I got a question."

"Spill it out then, *monsieur.*"

I shoved my face through the ivy for a better look.

"What the tarnation—"

"Tarnation? You must pardon me, *monsieur.* I am not familiar with this coarse American slang, if you please."

"What the *heck* were you talking about in that phone message you left?" Leonard grumbled. "You say only three hundred dollars for all this?"

"*Monsieur,* you ask too much of me. I've good-naturedly agreed to increase the original amount by one hundred dollars. What more do you want?" François threw his hands in the air. "As I've explained until I'm purple in the face, I simply cannot . . ."

His voice faded as he moved toward the far end of the patio. Leonard followed him, mumbling one-syllable replies. Before long they both were hunched over a table near the dining room entrance. François didn't seem angry anymore. In fact, he looked ecstatically happy. He started leaping around Leonard like a ballet dancer, gesturing wildly at whatever was on the table.

I didn't have a clear view, but I figured Leonard had dumped everything out of his Winn-Dixie bag, and it was the sight of all those Pitaya eggs that had François so tickled. I had to find out.

I pushed the gate.

Crrreak. I drew in a sharp breath and froze—not blinking an eyelash—until I was sure they hadn't heard me.

They kept talking. I slipped inside and dropped to my knees. Swiftly, silently, I crawled around the outer edge of the patio, darting from table to table until I got close to Leonard, François, and their pile of eggs.

"Is this not absolutely enchanting, *monsieur*?"

Really close . . .

"My lady of Paris will look stunning adorned with these rubies. Wouldn't you say so, my friend?"

So close . . . .

"*Voilà!* The vibrancy of color is out of this universe. Would not you agree?"

As Leonard mumbled an answer, my shoulder bumped into a chair, causing its legs to scrape against the concrete. François jerked his head back. "What is that noise?" he said, cupping a hand to his ear.

I dived under a nearby utility table. Luckily, it was covered with a long tablecloth. I took a shaky breath and peeked out from under it.

"*Mon Dieu!* It must be a rodent," François said. "I cannot tolerate those creatures in my establishment. I will check behind this buffet counter. You look under that tablecloth, *monsieur*. If we find it, I shall remove its head with my meat cleaver."

Clomp, clomp, clomp. Leonard's boots were headed straight toward me.

My heart stopped. My lungs froze. There was nowhere else to hide. In two seconds, I'd be face to face with Perpetrator Number One, Leonard Snout.

"Oh, for the sake of Peter," François said. "It must have been those cumbersome boots of yours scuffling about that I heard. Never mind, my friend. Now, back to our task at hand."

I gasped for air. When I finally had the nerve to peek out from my hiding spot again, Leonard and François had returned to the table. I still couldn't see what was on it.

By now I lay in a pool of sweat, my legs cramped and twitching. Where, where, where were Gus and Margaret? I was sure fifteen minutes had come and gone; they should've been here by now.

"If you please, *monsieur*, let us step inside a moment, in the comfort of air conditioning. I shall prepare us both an iced latte and then show you something of profound interest."

Leonard shrugged. He pulled off his dirty straw hat and tagged along after François.

The second they disappeared through the door, I whished out from under the table. I jumped up and ran to see what they'd been looking at, expecting to find the rest of the eggs, along with Mrs. Grimstone's heirlooms. I had the perfect plan, too. Since I had the locket with me, I'd hide it on the bottom of the stack so it would blend in with the other heirlooms—of course I'd have to scratch my picture out of it and replace it with Angel's, but I should have time to do that—and then I'd race back through the alley and find a phone and call the cops.

That was my plan, all right.

But it backfired.

Chapter 34
The Dirty Truth

I checked on top of the table, under the table, behind the table. Nothing. Not one piece of jewelry. No diamonds. No Pitayas. The closest thing I saw to an heirloom was a plastic spoon on the ground. What I did see, though, were stacks of landscaping magazines and pictures of patios and flower gardens— lots of them—along with an open notebook. My stomach did a nosedive when I recognized François' handwriting at the top of the page.

Patio Plan: A Flowering Extravaganza. Featuring the exotic, edible night-blooming pitaya—Belle Ruby!

Patio designed by François Pouppière.

(Implemented by Leonard Snout, under the guid-ance of François Pouppière).

All of a sudden a five-thousand-watt lightbulb exploded in my brain. I staggered backward. Because now I knew what this meeting was really about. And it didn't have the first thing to do with Mrs. Grimstone's heirlooms.

We'd been wrong. Wrong, wrong, wrong. So wrong I couldn't stand to think about it. François hadn't been planning a heist with Leonard. He'd been planning a flower garden for his patio.

I looked around. Dirt—tons of it—was shaped into little black mountains inside decorative brick hedges. Empty, ornamental flower pots were stacked everywhere. Concrete statues and fountains were lined against the patio fence. In the middle was a jeweled towering statue and on it, a plaque that said, THE EIFFEL TOWER, 1889: FRANÇOIS' LADY OF PARIS. And there were signs, gobs of them I hadn't noticed until now, scattered throughout the patio, popping out of every imaginable spot. Signs that said: PARDON OUR SOIL, PLEASE! A FLOWER/FOUNTAIN/AND SCULPTED PATIO GARDEN EXTRAORDINAIRE IS NEXT ON FRANÇOIS' MENU. IT WILL FEATURE OUR STUNNING, NIGHT-BLOOMING PITAYA.

The sound of voices startled me. They grew louder, with laughter sprinkled in.

I dropped on all fours again and scurried around the edge of the patio, like the giant dumb bunny I was. I headed straight for the gate. It locked behind me. I leaned against the fence to catch my breath. My face was seriously on fire, and it wasn't because of the scorching sun.

François and Leonard weren't crooks. The real crook was still on the loose, and the heirlooms— except for the locket and the egg—were long gone, and I was partly to blame.

I'd messed everything up by being so crazy over winning that reward, by not telling about the locket. If I'd turned it over to the cops right off the bat, maybe they could've found the real thief. And now *I* had the locket, burning a hole in my pocket. How could we return it to the police without telling the truth about what we'd been doing?

The worst thing of all was Granny Goose. We'd let her down. I still didn't doubt her innocence, not for a minute. But how could we prove anything now? Our suspect list was all washed up.

I sighed as I pulled myself up, wishing I felt half as happy as the accordion music coming from inside Simply Paris. I couldn't quit thinking about the stupid things I'd done over the last three days: eavesdropping on the Grimstones, calling Leonard, sneaking into François' office . . . it all brewed in my brain like a pot of burned coffee. I wanted to go home and crawl under my bed, hide from the world, but I had to wait for Gus and Margaret. I wiped the sticky sweat from my neck. What was taking them so long, anyway?

I headed down the alley to look for them. When I reached the back door of Shear Magic, my toe knocked against a container: SureFresh wintergreen mints, Cricket's brand. I hadn't noticed it earlier; she must've just come to the salon. I leaned over to pick it up, hoping to find a couple of leftover mints, when I saw a single key on the pavement next to the container. It was marked SHEAR MAGIC SUPPLY ROOM. I glanced at the salon's back door. It was opened partway. I pushed on it, thinking I should at least drop off the key.

I took a few steps into the short, dark hallway. Cricket was in the front by the receptionist's station, pacing the floor. Just as I started to call out to her, someone rapped on the salon's front window. "Brad!" Cricket yelled. She flew to the door, unlocked it, then threw her arms around the same blond guy she'd been with at the Tarts' tent on Thursday.

"What took you so long? Oh, my God, I'm a wreck! I thought you weren't going to make it back," she said, burying her face in his shoulder.

Brad locked the door behind him. "Calm down, babe. I told you I'd be back this morning. Everything's settled. My fence in Miami's going to take it all."

Fence?

I backed into the shadows of the hallway, my heart racing. Thanks to Gus and NSCCB, I knew what a fence was.

"What's going on?" Brad said. "My cell's about dead. You kept breaking up. You say they suspect the goose lady?"

Cricket started pacing again, running her hands through her spiked hair, rambling a million miles a minute: "It's crazy . . . doesn't make sense . . . two pieces gone . . . Unger's been questioned . . ."

"Slow down," Brad said. "Tell me what hap—"

"Someone's been in the shed. I think it's this kid Lindy."

Chapter 35
Shear Madness

My head spun as if a hurricane had just roared through it. Trembling, I gripped the handle of the shampoo cart. Me? In Cricket's shed? Where had she gotten that idea?

Brad reared his head back in surprise. "A kid? What the . . . Okay, take it from the beginning here, babe. You're saying a kid was in the shed? How? I locked it Thursday morning, right after we checked everything."

"She must've gotten in where those boards are missing on the side," Cricket said. "Her and her friends have been hanging around the neighborhood, acting weird. I think they're playing detective.

Anyway, a couple of pieces are missing from the duffel. One of the eggs ended up in Unger's turtle pen."

Brad let out a string of not so nice words, then said, "Missing boards? Man, Crick. I told you the shed was a lousy place to hide it."

"Quit blaming me," Cricket snapped. "How could I know? It's a small hole. I never expected anyone to crawl in there. And besides, you're the one who left the duffel out, not me. It was wide open on the floor. You told me you'd lock it back in the trunk."

Brad ran his hand through his hair. "Yeah? Well I didn't think it mattered. I assumed the shed was safe."

I stayed rooted to my spot behind the shampoo cart, barely breathing as they argued about what was whose fault, where the locket could be, why only two pieces were missing, how the egg had ended up at Granny Goose's.

"You should've been paying closer attention," Brad said. "You should've been checking on that bag."

"So I'm not perfect, all right!" Cricket yelled. "And why would I need to check on something that's locked inside a trunk anyway?" Her voice broke, like she was choking back a sob. I peeked around the cart. She gripped a sink basin, her chest heaving with every breath she took. "I've been here by myself since Thursday, having to kiss up to Mrs. Grimstone, make sure she doesn't suspect. I'm ready to crack."

"It's okay, babe. I know you're tense. " He put his arm around her. "Sorry I had to be on the road. But hey, I got everything taken care of, even our tickets. Besides, from what you said, it's not us the cops suspect. It's the goose lady. Looks like we lucked out; we're in the clear."

Cricket sniffled again and opened a SureFresh container. She stuck one in her mouth. "Yeah, except for that kid. What's she up to anyway?" She tossed the mint container on the counter. It clanged and fell to the floor.

Wait a minute . . .

The mint container.

Pickles had one of Cricket's mint containers earlier, outside the shed. Could that goose actually have—

"Have you seen the Lindy kid today?" Brad said.

"Yeah, earlier. She and her friends were nosing around Unger's house."

It's a small hole. I never expected anyone to crawl in there, Cricket had just said. Yes. It had to have been Pickles. The duffel was on the floor . . . open . . . she likes shiny things . . . *into everything,* Granny Goose had said.

"Man. If you're right and she's involved, we should get out of here. She could be talking to the cops right now. Let's get the stuff and go. Where'd you put the duffel?"

"It's locked in the supply room. Let me get my key to the door."

I fingered the bumpy ridge of the key in my hand, my heart pounding.

Unless Cricket had a backup key, she and Brad wouldn't be getting inside the supply room anytime soon. If I hurried, I could beat them to it.

Once I got my legs to move, I slunk along the wall to a closed door. I stuck the key in the lock, praying it would work. My hand was shaking so hard I could barely turn the handle.

Brad rapped his fingers on a sink basin. "Hurry it up, babe. We don't have all day."

"Hold on. I told you I'm looking."

The door opened.

I slipped inside and locked the dead bolt. Cricket and Brad were still in the front part of the salon, arguing. I should have a couple of minutes at least. I scanned the room, hoping the Shear Magic bag would jump out at me. Instead, all I saw were bottles of hair gel, mousse, hair spray, perm solutions, coloring kits, and nail polish, all neatly stacked on open shelves. I took a deep breath and started my search on the bottom, thinking I'd work my way up.

Three shelves higher, still no duffel. The only shelf left was the top one, but it was too high to reach. I dragged a box filled with cream rinses from across the room and stood on it. Yes! There it sat, against the wall, wedged between other containers. But when I tugged at it, my elbow knocked into a box of nail polish. I yelped as it flew off the shelf. About a thousand bottles of Pink Flamingo Flirt and Boys 'N Berry Passion crashed to the ground. They spun and bounced and rolled all over the floor.

I stood absolutely still, petrified, hugging the duffel bag to my chest. I had to get out of there, quick. But if I went back through the hall to the exit, Cricket and Brad might see me. I stared across the room at my only other option, a tiny window about six feet from the floor. Could I manage to wriggle through it?

Something thumped against the supply room door. I swallowed a scream as the doorknob turned. Back and forth, back and forth.

"Hurry up with the key," Brad yelled. "I heard something back here."

I quickly pushed the cream rinse box toward the window; it wasn't high enough. I'd need a second box if I wanted to make it outside. I started back to the shelves but tripped over a bottle of nail polish and fell to the floor.

By now Brad was slamming himself against the door.

"Hold on!" Cricket shouted. "I'll look in the register."

Brad muttered some more choice words, then wriggled the doorknob again. I forced myself up, grabbed the second box, and scrambled for the window. It was opened partway. Maybe I could push the screen out.

I climbed on top of the boxes. No luck. The window was way too small for me to fit through.

Any hope I had of escaping faded. I was just about to start bawling and wailing and begging for Cricket's mercy when I heard something.

A honk?

I heard it again. Yes, most definitely a goose honk. That meant Margaret and Gus must be right outside.

I craned my neck and peeked out the tiny window. Margaret and Pickles weren't more than three feet away from me.

"Psst," I hissed as loud as possible.

Margaret looked up. Her jaw dropped into her neck. "Lindy?"

I blinked back the salty tears stinging my eyes. "Where's Gus? Does he have the cell phone?" My voice sounded hoarse, frantic.

"He's coming down the alley by François' kitchen. We split up because we didn't want to miss you. He forgot the phone in his saxophone case. What's wrong?" Her eyes looked big and scared.

From behind me, Brad yelled at Cricket to "hurry up already before I bash the *blankety-blank* door in."

"Wh-What's going on, Lindy?" Margaret whispered.

"How come you need the phone? Is someone else in there?"

I nodded. "Find François. Use his phone and call the police. Hurry!"

"François? But he's a—"

"He's not the crook. Cricket is, and she's got a partner." I pushed the screen out, dropping the duffel bag at Margaret's feet. "Take that. The heirlooms are in it. Oh, and this, too." I tossed the locket to her.

Margaret's eyes nearly popped from their sockets. "*Cricket*? Ohmigosh! Where is she? Are you trapped?"

Pickles squawked again, and an idea hit me. "Give me Pickles." I reached my arms out the window.

"I found it!" Cricket yelled.

Margaret stared up at me, openmouthed, like a scream was forming in the back of her throat.

"Hurry," I said. "I need her."

Margaret lifted her up to the window, and Pickles

clucked a little greeting, like she was happy to see me.

"Go now," I said. Margaret grabbed the bag and the locket, then sailed down the alley toward Simply Paris, her fiery curls bouncing in the sunlight.

Outside the supply room door, Cricket said, "Here. Use this."

There was nowhere to hide. I sank to the floor, holding Pickles to my chest, then closed my eyes and waited.

Chapter 36
Someone Please Call 911!

The key clicked in the lock.

I kept my head down, eyes closed. For some reason, the darkness felt safer.

Pickles cooed on my lap. My arms tensed around her. The door creaked.

"Watch out, Brad," Cricket muttered. "Someone's on the floor. Over there."

My eyes inched open. Brad stared at me from the doorway.

Cricket shoved him aside. When she recognized me, her face darkened. "You? What're you—"

"Oh, thank goodness you heard me!" I said,

faking a sniffle. "I'm watching Mrs. Unger's goose today, and she got loose. She ran in the back door of your salon, and I chased her into this room. Then wham! The door locked behind me. We've been so scared. We, uh . . . didn't know what to d-do." I wiped my eyes and snorted into the crook of my elbow. "Did we, Pickles?"

"Why, you little . . . " Cricket started after me, but Pickles cackled and honked and snapped at her.

"Aaaagh!" Cricket screamed, ducking behind Brad. "Oh, my God! That goose terrifies me. Get it out of here."

"Stay cool, babe. I'll take care of this," Brad said.

He took a couple of steps toward me and Pickles. I sniveled some more, squeezing fat tears from my eyes. "Please don't hurt the goose. It's not her fault she's acting so wild. She's just upset because Mrs. Unger got thrown in jail."

"What?" Cricket's eyes narrowed. "She's in jail?"

"Oh, haven't you heard?" I said. "Mrs. Grimstone

was right. It turned out Granny Goose was the heirloom thief. The police arrested her at the festival. I saw them. That's why I'm taking care of Pickles."

Brad looked at Cricket, a sly smile on his face. Had he believed me?

"I don't trust her," Cricket said, shooting sparks at me with her eyes. "And look." She pointed at the top shelf. "The duffel's gone." She kicked a bunch of nail polish bottles. They spun across the floor toward me, causing Pickles to honk again.

I glanced up at the window. Where were Gus and Margaret?

"Okay, kid," Brad said. "No games here. You need to give us the duffel. Now."

"Oh?" I acted surprised. "Do you mean that brown bag with Shear Magic embroidered on it?"

"Yeah," Brad said. "That one."

"I don't have it. Honest. Your, uh, receptionist has it."

A look of panic crossed Cricket's face. "Marcy?"

"Yeah, that's her," I lied, and my heart bounced around my chest like a Ping-Pong ball. I had to stall them until Margaret found help. "She was out back in the alley when I came after Pickles. She was acting kind of strange, you know, like she was in a really big hur—"

"Shut up!" Cricket said, then turned to Brad. "She's lying." She tore through the supply room, tossing packages aside, checking under boxes, searching the shelves. "Where . . . is . . . it?"

"I swear I'm not lying." I scrambled up from the floor, clinging to Pickles, but she was getting restless and hard to hold. "Marcy has it."

"I said shut your mouth." Cricket pulled Brad aside and whispered something to him.

He looked my way and nodded, and icy fear hit me like a stun gun, freezing every organ in my body.

Luckily, Pickles wasn't frozen . . .

Chapter 37
Tongs and Shovels and Bad Guys

Pickles went berserk, squawking, hissing, screeching, snapping. She broke out of my arms, landed on the floor, then lit into Cricket's ankles.

Cricket kicked at her, screaming like a banshee, "Kill it! Kill it, Brad!"

Brad swore and lunged for Pickles, but I snatched her first. I flew out of the room and escaped through the back door of Shear Magic, panting for breath.

"*Mon Dieu!*" came a cry from down the alley. "It's the girl and the goose."

François?

I swung around, nearly fainting with relief. My rescue team was on its way: François waving cooking utensils, Leonard lugging a shovel, and my two best friends, whirling toward me like a wind gust.

Brad started off across the alley. "Stop, crook!" François shouted. He dived toward Brad, swatting at him with his tongs.

Then Leonard took over. He grabbed Brad's shoulder, shoved him to the ground, and held him in place with the shovel. "I got him now," Leonard said. "He ain't going nowhere."

"But the Cricket?" François said, looking all around. "She has escaped, *n'est-ce pas?*"

"In Sh-Shear Magic," I said, still trying to catch my breath. "She may be trying to get out the front."

"Aha!" François clicked his tongs together. "I'll be back."

Margaret scooped Pickles up, and then she, Gus, and I ran after François. He'd managed to corner Cricket by the front door. When she saw us and realized she couldn't get away, she slid down the wall and buried her face in her hands, crying.

And that's when the cop car pulled up in front of the salon.

An hour or so later, after the cops had taken Brad and a sobbing Cricket to the station, a bunch of us were still gathered on François' patio: Margaret's parents, my parents, Gus's dad, Leonard, Pickles, and some other townspeople who'd already heard the news.

"Whatever were you thinking?" Mom said for the fiftieth time. "Why on earth didn't you tell us . . . What in God's name did you expect . . ." Scold, scold, scold. She hadn't left my side since Dad, Henry, and she had run in the front door of Simply Paris.

My dad still looked a little shaken, as if he'd just put out a five-alarm fire. He hadn't said much, only a few stern statements like "Don't ever pull a stunt like this again" and "We'll talk some more about this at home."

Henry, on the other hand, treated me like a rock star. "Did you really catch a thief, Lindy?" he kept asking me, until Mom hushed him.

Margaret got the same kind of reaction from her parents. I couldn't tell what Gus's dad was thinking, except his eyes seemed to shine with pride when the captain of the police force shook our hands.

François flitted from table to table, taking drink orders and boasting about his role in the capture of Cricket and Brad.

"*Mon Dieu!*" he said, putting his hand to his heart. "When I thought that child was in danger, *madame*, my adrenaline began to steam. To my fiancée, I said, 'You call the police, Greta, and I shall go after the girl. She may be near the door of death.'

"Thank heavens," François said. "I succeeded in frightening that villain senseless with my tongs, or I and these children would surely have been minced into meat by him. *Oui*, he was a wild one, but . . ."

He was still boasting as I finally got away from the crowd with Margaret and Gus. We found a table on the far side of the patio. "I can't believe it," Margaret said. "I thought for sure François and Leonard were the thieves. Just think, Lindy. You might've been kidnapped if Gus and I hadn't shown up at the right time."

"The right time? Are you serious? You guys were supposed to have been there lots earlier. How come it took you so long?"

"Well," she said, "the first thing is that the sound system broke down again, right after you left. It took them ten more minutes to fix it. And then, well . . ."

Gus's face turned red. "Uh, it's kind of my fault. I kept, uh . . ."

"Squeaking," Margaret said. They started talking at the same time, telling me how Angel had a total meltdown on the stage because of Gus's squeaking.

"No one could hear her during the trio part," Margaret said.

"It turns out my reed was split," Gus said. "So Mr. Austin stopped the whole concert to get me a new one, and then, uh, something else happened, and we couldn't get out of there."

"What else?"

"This part is my fault," Margaret said. "Right when Mr. Austin handed Gus the new reed, Pickles pooped on Mrs. Grimstone's shoe."

"Really?" I put both hands to my mouth, laughing. "How did that happen?"

"Remember how I had Pickles tied next to the stage?" Margaret said. "Mrs. Grimstone was sitting in the front row so she could get pictures of Angel, and Pickles's leash was a little longer than I thought . . ."

"It held up the whole show," Gus said. "We had to clean it up and tie Pickles somewhere else, and then we got back onstage, and I, uh—"

"Kept squeaking!" Margaret said.

"Yeah." Gus shook his head. "The whole thing was kind of like a comedy of errors."

"It might've been a comedy for you guys," I said, "but . . ." I'm not sure why—maybe it was something like posttraumatic stress syndrome, or the thought of the fun they'd had without me again, of the squeaking and Angel's temper tantrum and the goose poop—but a tear almost pushed its way out of my eye. I sniffled and wiped my hand across my face. "For me, it wasn't funny at all. It was like being in a horror show."

Then, to my surprise, another tear popped out and trickled down my cheek. And all I could do was sit there, thinking what a big crybaby I must look like.

Chapter 38
Forgotten Heart

Margaret jumped out of her chair and wrapped her arms around me. "I'm sorry, Lindy. Gosh, I would've been scared, too, if I were you."

"We really wanted to get over here," Gus said, "more than anything. I kind of panicked when I had Mr. Austin breathing down my neck, Angel crying, everyone laughing at me. I thought you'd be safe, you know, just spying on Leonard and François from the alley. If I'd known about the trouble you were in, I would've jumped off the stage and run right over here."

"Me, too," Margaret said, wiping her eyes. "Gosh,

Lindy. You're my very best friend. I'd never want you to get hurt."

Her very best friend?

I grinned and elbowed her in the side. "It's okay. The important thing is, we proved Granny Goose wasn't the thief. Right?"

"Right," Margaret said. "And all her animals still have their home. Maybe she can even get François to help her come up with a recipe to win that cook-off contest, too. That way she can expand the rescue service."

"Uh, yeah, maybe," I said. But no way was I going to be the taste tester.

"So how'd you do it?" Gus asked me. "I mean, how'd you figure out Cricket was the perp? At least ninety-nine-point-nine percent of the evidence pointed to François and Leonard. Man. I'm gonna run all this by the NSCCB, see what their take on it is."

"The evidence *did* point to them," Margaret said. "Especially all that stuff in the planner. I don't get it."

"Actually, François was talking about landscaping," I said. "He's hired Leonard to plant a flower garden, right here on this patio."

Margaret's hand flew to her mouth. "A flower garden? You mean, that's all it was?"

Gus pulled the planner from his pocket and started thumbing through it. "Aah. That explains the entry about *L* getting to work early. Who's *G*, though?"

"It's Greta, François' fiancée," I whispered. "She's the one who thought I was the Cucumber Princess. I wonder if the thing about diamonds has something to do with an engagement ring."

"But then what about the Pitayas?" Margaret said. "How come François talked about them?"

"He wasn't talking about the jeweled eggs," I said, pointing to one of François' signs. "He was talking about a flower called pitaya. Leonard's supposed to plant a bunch of them back here."

So then I told them everything that happened at

Shear Magic and how I'd overheard Cricket and Brad. "That's when I knew it was Pickles."

Margaret looked at me blankly. "Pickles?"

"Boy, that was a long shot," Gus said. "The odds of animal involvement is only four percent."

"NSCCB?" I said.

Gus nodded.

Margaret threw her hands up, waving them all around. "Wait a minute, you guys. Pickles *isn't* the robber."

I laughed. "Don't worry. No one's going to arrest a goose. But actually, she *is* the one who framed Granny Goose." And then I explained how Pickles had gotten into the shed, found the open duffel bag, and helped herself to the locket and egg. "Remember how she had Granny Goose's serving spoon? She likes shiny stuff."

"There they are!" a voice boomed. Granny Goose whooshed toward us, her arms outstretched. The next thing I knew I was smothered in her bear hug, hardly able to breathe. Pickles danced around our feet, squawking and fussing for Granny Goose's attention.

"Hold on to your feathers," Granny Goose scolded her. "I'll get to you in a minute. I've got to tell these kids how much I appreciate them."

She moved around the table, hugging Margaret and Gus and then me again. "You nabbed 'em," she said. "You flat-out nabbed the scoundrels, and if it hadn't been for you, I'd be stewing my cucumbers at the city jail. Why, I can't believe it. You three kids have more sense than the whole darn police department." She turned to Officer Moore, who'd followed her over to our table. "Isn't that right, Frank? Looks like you could use some tips from these youngsters."

I heard a snort behind us. Leonard was on the ground, digging in the dirt as he stared at Granny Goose. His face crinkled into a smile.

"Uh-hum." Officer Moore turned the color of strawberry soda. "I have to say we owe a big round of thanks to these kids."

"Wish I could've been there, honey," Granny Goose said to me. "I would've knocked the socks off that Brad character. What's going to happen to Cricket and the boyfriend anyway?" she asked Officer Moore.

Another snort from Leonard, who seemed to be digging his way toward our table. I watched him for a couple of seconds. How come we'd been so scared of him anyway? He didn't seem all that bad. It looked like Pickles was making up to him, too. She waddled his way, and he reached out to pet her.

Officer Moore continued. "I'd like you all to know that Cricket Schaeffer has confessed. Charges will be brought against the two of them. Her boyfriend, Brad Myers, has a rap sheet longer than my arm. He'll be facing some serious time."

"Such a brute, that man," François said. He turned to Officer Moore, lowering his voice. "But it is the lovely Mrs. Grimstone who has my sympathies at this moment, *monsieur*. Tell me, please, is she aware of my surprising attack on the criminal and of my role in the safe return of her heirlooms?"

Officer Moore turned his head slightly and coughed into his fist, but not before his upper lip twitched. Either he was holding in a sneeze, or he'd caught on to François as quick as I had. "Yes," he said with a straight face. "I believe Mrs. Grimstone is aware of everything that happened today, and she sends her sincere thanks to all involved."

"Who cares about her thanks?" I whispered in Margaret's ear. "All I want is the reward." We smothered our laughter with napkins.

Officer Moore looked at me, his left eyebrow arched. "There is one thing puzzling Mrs. Grimstone. Her granddaughter discovered something odd about one of the recovered pieces."

I sat straight up, feeling the color drain from my face. Oops. How could I have forgotten that tiny detail?

Chapter 39

Grand Finale = The Trio Triumphs

I reached in my pocket and pulled out the photo of Angel playing her flute. "Umm," I said, holding it up for Officer Moore to see. "Could this have anything to do with the puzzle?"

"Hey!" Henry said. "That picture came from the heart I found in our garage."

"A heart in our garage? What on earth are you kids talking about?" My mom leaned over to get a look at the photo in my hand. "Why, that's Angel Grimstone's picture." She narrowed her eyes at me. "I think you have some more explaining to do here, young lady."

Margaret jumped up from her seat. "It's all my fault, Mrs. Phillips. Really. I begged Lindy to hide the locket after we found it in the cucumbers because I was scared everyone would blame Granny Goo—I mean, Mrs. Unger, for stealing the heirlooms, and then we put it in your garage behind the Grubb's grime remover because Lindy said her dad wouldn't see it there because he never cleans anything. But Henry found it and—"

"Okay." Officer Moore cleared his throat again. "Let's take it slow and easy, kids. From the beginning, please."

"Actually," Gus said, "it all began with the goose . . ."

Of course Gus got top billing in the next day's headlines:

LOCAL BOY, TWO GIRLS, AND A GOOSE CRACK HEIR-LOOM CASE.

I didn't really care, though. The important

things were that Granny Goose was back home with Pickles and Doris and the gang, the heirlooms had been returned to their rightful owners, and Mrs. Grimstone made good on her reward offer. We didn't exactly get a big presentation ceremony at City Hall, like I'd hoped, but along with our families, we did get a special invitation to the Grimstones' house.

"I would like to thank the three of you," Mrs. Grimstone said in front of everyone. She handed me a check for $4,788. "As you can see," she explained, pointing to the amount, "Howard and I have subtracted the cost of Angel's princess gown. Such an unfortunate waste of money that was. My maids were unable to remove the strawberry stains."

"Oh, um, sorry about that," I muttered.

"What's done is done," she said, waving her hand at me. "Believe me, the loss of that gown pales to the devastation I've endured over the turn of events with Cricket." She dabbed her eyes with a hankie and turned to her husband. "Honestly,

Howard. How could I have been so careless with details regarding our valuables? I feel such a fool for my poor judge of character."

Mr. Grimstone put his arm around her shoulder. "There, there, dear," he said. "Don't blame yourself for this. You had no way of knowing Cricket's intent or that she had such unsavory acquaintances."

"Well, both of them will certainly pay for their actions," my mom said. "I imagine they'll receive a few years in prison, at the very least. And I'm terribly sorry, Hazel, for the way Cricket betrayed your trust. That must've been quite a letdown."

"Indeed!" Mrs. Grimstone said. "And to imagine that thug boyfriend of hers cavorting about our home! Why, I'm not even sure when or how he entered. It must've been during the soufflé presentation. You know, we had so many people in here— thirty, at the least—that I wasn't able to keep track of all the comings and goings. And not one of my help noticed anything untoward."

"Yep," Mr. Grimstone said, pulling a fresh cigar out of his shirt pocket. "A real lowlife, that fellow. I'm relieved to know he's behind bars."

Once my share of the money was deposited in the bank, we had a family meeting about how it would be spent. It seemed like my plans were way different from my parents'.

"Band camp and a new flute," I said.

"I vote for savings bonds," my dad said.

"A good, sensible idea," Mom said, like the case was closed.

It took three solid days of finagling and begging to get them to say okay to a new flute, especially since they weren't so thrilled with what Mom called my "questionable behavior." Band camp was still up in the air when we got a visit from Gus's dad. I overheard my parents talking to him in the kitchen.

"You're absolutely right," Mr. Kinnard said, after listening to my mom rant about the folly and danger of our actions and how her daughter "could've been hauled off to Timbuktu by Cricket and that sleazy boyfriend."

"I agree, these kids need to face some consequences for their actions. How about a couple of weeks' work on the school grounds? I understand the maintenance crew is doing a major landscaping job—I believe the gardener who worked for Mrs. Grimstone is supervising it—and they could use summer help."

"That's an excellent idea," Mom said. "Lindy needs some structure this summer."

"I'll call the necessary people and arrange it," Mr. Kinnard said. "And thanks for agreeing to let Lindy attend camp. I'm grateful to her and Margaret for the friendship they've shown Gus over the last few days. It's the happiest I've seen him since his mother died."

Actually, the whole landscaping thing didn't turn out so bad. Leonard didn't hate us nearly as much as I thought, and he seemed happier working for the city than he did the Grimstones. He even taught us a lot about flowers, like how the pitaya is a night-blooming edible plant that François planned to feature at Simply Paris. "He wants to place them around some fake Eiffel Tower in the middle of his patio," Leonard said.

After our last morning of work with Leonard, Margaret, Gus, and I headed over to Granny Goose's. She was throwing a going-away-to-camp-party in our honor. A lot of people would be there, she'd told us, including her veterinarian son from Orlando.

"He's moving back to Bloomsberry," Granny Goose had said. "He and his wife are tired of living in the city. They want to help with the rescue operation."

We turned down Main Street, talking about everything that'd happened in the last couple of weeks, when Angel and her friends walked out of the White Mountain Ice Creamery.

"Yoo-hoo, Mr. Sexy-phone," Angel yelled. "I bet

I know what you bought with my grammy's reward money."

"Oh, really?" I said. "How'd you ever guess he got you a muzzle?"

"Shut up. You're the one that needs a muzzle. Hey," Angel said to her friends, "did you hear that Mr. Sexy-phone bought both of his girlfriends a promise ring at the dollar shop?"

Lisa and Caroline giggled. Gus stiffened beside me. He drew in a deep breath and faced Angel. "Yep. That's what I got them, all right—solid-gold promise rings. You must be psychic or something."

"You mean *psychotic*," Margaret said.

"Yeah," I said, "as in lamebrain."

Angel shouted a bunch more insults at us, but I didn't care. I don't think Gus did either, because by the time we got half a block away, we were talking and laughing about other things. And once we'd made it to Granny Goose's house, Angel Grimstone was ancient history.

At the bottom of Granny Goose's porch steps I came to a dead stop. My nose started twitching. The unmistakable aroma of stewed cucumbers wafted from her front door. I shrugged my shoulders and sighed. I'd have to fake a stomach virus, because I definitely wasn't up for that snotball-in-my-throat feeling again.

Margaret skipped up the steps and ran inside to greet Pickles and Doris and Petunia the parrot, and everyone else that lived there. Gus stood beside me on the front porch, his cowlick sticking straight up. His T-shirt was stained, he had a smudge of something on his cheek, and I wasn't even 100 percent sure his shoes matched.

I grinned at him. "Hey. After the cucumber party, maybe you and Margaret can get your instruments and come back to my house. We'll work on scales. We need to prepare for the governor's concert."

"Yeah. That'd be great. Except there's about a ninety-eight percent chance I'm gonna squeak—just wanted to warn you."

"That's okay," I said, and I meant it.

"Look!" Margaret squealed from inside. She had something tiny and fuzzy and brown cuddled against her chest. "Look what Granny Goose is giving me. Ohmigosh! Isn't it the most adorable thing you ever saw? It's a goosling."

"You mean gosling," Gus said. "A baby goose is a gos—"

"Don't you want one, too, Lindy?"

"Umm, maybe." I watched Margaret dance around the living room, cooing over the gosling, kissing its fuzzy head. Her face beamed with happiness.

"You know what," I said to Gus. "Instead of practicing scales, let's look for another trio, one that we can play at the fall concert."